Twisted Minds

August Knights MC

Book #1

The Twisted Series

By:

Keta Kendric

Cover: Steamy Designs
Editing: Tammy Jernigan

ISBN: 978-1-956650-12-9/Twisted Minds

Contents

Synopsis

Megan: How the hell did I end up here on a heavily wooded road in the middle of a racist county, all alone with nothing but my twisted mind for protection? After convincing the August Knights Motorcycle Club to allow me to work off a debt my sister owed them, I found myself in the middle of madness and mayhem. I should've known that this was what life inside this dangerous club would be like, right?

Aaron: How the hell did I end up here? I was face to face and chest to chest with the one woman I was forbidden to touch. Strange, sexy, inexplicably delicious, and just downright twisted events began to unfold when I met Megan. I can't figure her out, but there is one thing she can't hide—her attraction to me. When Megan wiggles her way into my life, I discover that her quiet, good-girl persona is a cloak she uses to hide the twisted mind she harbors. A mind just as bent as mine.

Warning
Please be advised. This book is a multicultural romance that contains explicit sexual content and is intended for adults. If you are easily triggered by morally grey characters, explicit language and graphic violence, this is not the book for you.

INTRODUCTION

I must have been born under a haze of gun smoke, surrounded by a slew of dead bodies during a deadly shootout. Born August Aaron Knox V, into a life of madness and murder, I couldn't, nor have I ever tried to outrun the trouble I inherited, or the mayhem embedded in my DNA. I embraced this life I was given and even found easier, faster ways to cause and get out of trouble.

A member of the August Knights Motorcycle Club, I became the club's enforcer years ago due to my brutal nature and unapologetic attitude. I've never known what it was like to live a normal, worry-free life. I reckon it was a pretty boring-ass existence.

Instinctively, I ducked. A bullet whizzed past my face, yanking me out of my head. It pounded into the concrete cinder block over my right shoulder, causing chunks to fly up and pepper the skin on the back of my neck.

I brushed pieces from my shoulder-length hair and aim my attention in the direction of the fired shot.

Actively engaged in a gunfight, I was more irritated at being shot at than I feared being shot. My anger flared, surging through me and making the veins in my forehead pulse.

The New York gang currently attacking us had sadly underestimated the amount of danger they were set to face when dealing with me and the people with whom I conducted business.

I was a well-behaved guest of the city for nearly a week while waiting for the shipment of guns from my supplier. We planned these exchanges beforehand to ensure a smooth transition, operating in several covert locations across five states that we picked at random.

Up until now, the planning worked, keeping unwanted attention away. This location, which we would no longer be able to use, was somehow leaked to this local New York gang.

"Max, cut the fucking lights," I barked through gritted teeth to one of my crewmen. Apparently, the gang of about eight assumed they could steal a shipment of guns worth two million dollars. What they hadn't counted on was us being ready for them or that my supplier would protect the product from start to drop.

The delivery men were armed and ready. They remained with me for protection and would stay now until I released them. Plus, I always brought at least a three-man crew of my own and we always packed the kind of heat that could make it rain fire and pour blood.

Within seconds, Max made the lights in the underground parking structure we'd used for the past two years go black. My men knew if I called for a blackout, we were going full-on black ops with night gear.

Many of my associates, business partners, and I were ex-military, so this gang was so far in over their heads they were better off putting a bullet in their own brains.

Once the lights were out, the shuffling and screeching of tennis shoes was easily distinguished inside the echo-inducing garage. The whisper of nervous commands versus the dead silence of my crew told of our vast differences. The silencers we had on our pistols spoke volumes about our criminal professionalism versus theirs.

Four minutes and five of the gang members were already dead. Three remained. Make it two. I just splattered one's brains all over his buddy's clean white T-shirt. Who the fuck wears a white T-shirt at night during an attempted robbery?

The act of putting a bullet in someone and watching their worthless body cling to the last remnants of life calmed my anger considerably.

"We need to keep one alive," I said to my group in a low, easy voice. "Make that alive enough for him to get the message back to his crew."

"Got it."

"Okay."

"Yep."

My men were spread throughout the garage, acknowledging my words. Their responses sounded off, loud and clear in my earpiece.

This immature gang was slowing down my progress and losing their lives because they were too damn dumb and impatient to execute a well-thought-out plan. I had better shit to do with my time, like getting these guns to the people who were waiting for them.

I approached and stood over the last surviving member. The sound of the lights flipping back on echoed throughout the sub-basement level of the huge structure.

Big, terrified, gray eyes stared at me as blood oozed from a knife wound in the man's shoulder and from the gunshot to his shattered kneecap.

His top teeth ground into the bottom and pain poured off of him like toxic fumes. My blue-eyed gaze was cast down on the injured man like dark, hovering shadows.

"Tell your people the next time they interfere in the August Knights Motorcycle Club's business, they will be paid a visit."

I snapped my fingers in front of the man's face when his heavy eyes fluttered like broken wings on his face. "Focus, motherfucker!" I yelled. He snapped up, his gaze widening as he shook his head vigorously.

"You remember the Crimson Hill Gang?" I asked him.

He shook his head, denying knowing the gang.

"Exactly. Their gang disbanded because we killed twenty of those motherfuckers in one night. CHG no longer exists because they fucked with the wrong group." I shook my pistol in front of the man's saucer wide eyes to reinforce my comments. "A bit of advice. Always know who you're fucking with before you fuck with them."

Just to fuck with him, I cast cold, dead eyes down on him for a half minute just to watch him squirm.

"Based on that tattoo on your arm, you're one of the Elm Street Kings. Your gang has been around for about seven years. Your main crew consists of about seventy members, minus the ones who have carelessly gotten themselves killed here tonight. You claim Elm Street, but most of you live in Maple Grove."

The man's eyes had grown wide enough to bulge from the sockets. He no longer cared about his injuries. His dread-filled gaze remained locked with mine. His face paled like he'd seen a ghost and his wide eyes searched mine, likely wondering how the hell I knew so much about his gang.

I shook my head but didn't vocalize what was rolling through it. *That's right, motherfucker, I do my homework, and you should have done yours.* If the poor bastard had any good sense, he'd heed my words because I didn't give a damn about killing him and every member of his gang.

CHAPTER ONE

Megan

"You must be lost."

The rough voice boomed through my driver's side window as I was parking my white rental car. The voice came from a biker straight off a Hollywood set. His long black beard didn't match his stringy brown hair. He stood well over six feet, wearing black jeans, a leather biker's vest, and black boots. He leaned against his Harley with his ankles crossed, staring at me with curious amusement shining in his gaze.

Peering through my windshield, I swept the area surrounding what I assumed was their motorcycle club. The clubhouse sat far back off a quiet highway nearly surrounded by woods. Initially, I'd driven past the building that resembled a double-wide mobile home at first glance.

When I drove closer, I discovered that it was an old wooden homestead with peeling white paint that the bikers had turned into their clubhouse. "Club" was painted in big dripping black letters above the entrance door.

The dirty and unsavory looking bikers milling about all possessed similarly tall, muscular builds, wore jeans, and black leather vests that showcased their MC's logo on the back.

The logo was a fully armored knight, riding a steel horse. Instead of a sword, he carried a machine gun with two additional guns strapped to his back.

Inquisitive gazes zoomed in on me as I cut the engine and contemplated opening my door to approach the shabby white building. Out of my element was an understatement. There were no words to describe my level of freaked out. My twisted mind was a river of chaos and it had set me on a path to engage with these bikers. I was all out of options and desperation had led me here.

After rolling up my window and exiting my vehicle, I slinked past bikers who stopped what they were doing to gape in my direction. My purse strap was my unsteady anchor as I gripped it in my clenched fist.

Everyone outside the clubhouse stopped whatever they were doing to gawk, making me the center of attention. Fingers began to point, and faces frowned as I ambled closer to the club's entrance on shaky legs. Open-mouthed expressions, pinched brows, and evil stares followed me as I reached for the door. If I were being honest with myself, I hadn't expected to make it this far.

The tremble in me intensified, forcing me to keep down the sandwich I forced myself to eat earlier. Sweat drizzled down my back, and I was sure it wasn't the late June heat causing it.

I was afraid. No, fuck that. I was scared shitless, but my need to rectify a life-altering situation that loomed at my back was greater than my fears. Unfortunately, for me, there were worse things than subjecting myself to a bunch of racist bikers. I kept repeating the comment in my head, but it did nothing to calm the anxiety crackling through me.

Even as my heart threatened to punch the hell out of my ribs to break out of my chest, I forced myself to proceed with my plan. I pulled the door open and entered the club, praying with each shaky step that I could make my plan work.

The floorboards creaked under each of my wobbly steps and sounded like rolling thunder despite the noise of the group inside. The door didn't close behind me because the group I assumed I left outside held it open and peeked into the club after me.

When I spotted the man I was searching for, I approached calling out to him.

"Mr. Shark?" I asked in a low, passive tone.

"Who the fuck is asking?" The biker slung the question in my direction, his voice filled with bass, before he turned to face me. His penetrating blue-eyed gaze locked with my gaping brown eyes. A face laced with distaste and alarming hate swept down my body and back up .

"My name is Megan Jones. I'm—"

"Speak up!" he snapped.

I jumped damn near out of my skin. The air around me grew thicker inside the dingy dive. The air-conditioning unit buzzed with life as voices quieted to low murmurs. The whine of country music sounded from someplace in the background.

It was just as hot inside this place as the ninety-two-degree Florida heat outside. When the piercing, blue-eyed menace I'd disturbed raised his voice and told me to speak up, all eyes jetted in our direction from every corner of the large, dusty room. It wasn't hard to decide that the eyes that probed me belonged to a group who was not used to seeing the likes of me.

I cleared my throat and clamped my unsteady hands together. Murmurs and not-so-hushed voices sounded. The group was no longer talking about whose mufflers on their oversized trucks roared the loudest or how many times their motorcycle engines had been rebuilt. I was a much more interesting subject for them to discuss.

"Who the fuck is this black bitch?" a voice called out over the crowd of about twenty, scattered throughout the bar.

"What the fuck does she want?" another asked.

"Does she not know where the fuck she's at?"

I did my best to ignore the questions being lobbed in my direction. An African American woman walking into a known racist motorcycle club wasn't something that occurred every day. It wasn't something that any sane person attempted.

"My name is Megan Jones," I stated again to the biker I presumed was Shark. I craned my neck up to see his bearded face. "I'm here on behalf of my sister, Jennifer. She took drugs from your club on credit and didn't pay you on time." I paused to swallow enough fear to keep talking as the menacing glare of the mean biker seared me down to my quaking bones.

"Your men chased my sister down and promised to kill her if she didn't pay what she owed them. I'm here to see if I can repay you for her mistake."

The towering biker loomed. Middle-aged, he was bearded with a long scar over his left cheek. He didn't say anything. Just stared, seemingly through me. His dark hair was cut low to his skull, which was unexpected since I lumped every biker into the long-dirty-oily-haired category. His deep-set, blue eyes bore flashes of the hard life he led.

His arms were a canvas of tattoos that likely continued under the leather vest and black T-shirt he paired with well-worn jeans and black boots. I'd learned through studying what I could find out about this organization that the president of the August Knights Motorcycle Club was named August Knox IV and was called Shark.

He tilted his head and glanced around me, undoubtedly expecting the army I must have with me.

"Sir, I can assure you, I'm alone," I confirmed. My words were as shaky as my body. "I want to make things right with you so that your men won't hurt my sister."

Without saying anything the tall biker glanced around the area. He stood abruptly, staring and no doubt wondering if I was crazy enough to do what I was attempting to do. He took a step closer, and I inched back.

"Are you one of them escaped crazies or something?" he asked, leaning closer to get a better look into my eyes. He probably assumed I was high or drunk.

Eyeing me suspiciously from head to toe, he was close enough for his warm breath to brush my face. Other than nodding to answer his question, I didn't move any part of my fear-frozen body.

"I'm not crazy. I came to see if I could pay my sister's debt. I don't have a lot of money, so I'm willing to pay you in installments if you'll allow it."

I swallowed the brick-size lump in my throat and quickly sucked in a huge gust of air when the big biker strong-armed me. My tennis shoes squeaked against the dirty, brown linoleum floor as I struggled for balance.

My eyes bulged from their sockets as he backed me up and gripped my tense shoulders before he slammed me into the wall behind us. My anxious fingers scraped the particle board wall I was harshly introduced to.

Pain registered, but my true fight was to not pass out from fear. The music in the background halted, tones hushed, feet stopped shuffling, and interested gazes zoomed in on Shark and me.

"Who the fuck are you?" he asked. His sharp glare warned me not to fuck with him. "You better be lost or crazy because you have stumbled into the wrong club. Don't you know this is a *whites-only* establishment? There aren't any signs posted, but anybody around here who don't live under a fucking rock knows that fact."

My voice cracked when I attempted to reply. I squeezed my eyes shut so tight water oozed from between my lids as I fought against the pain of the tight grip Shark had on my shoulders. I balanced on the balls of my feet because he'd hiked me up the wall a couple of notches.

"Mr. Shark. I'm who I say I am. I'm here to square my sister's debt. She's on drugs, and I'm usually left to clean up the messes she makes. I checked her into rehab and now I'm here to try to do right by you and your men on her behalf, so..."

I was losing it. I'd promised myself I'd do this with bravery, but I was so damn scared, I was losing what little courage that remained to tears. Swallowing hard, I found my voice. "...so your men won't come after her again and kill her."

My nerves taunted me so harshly I babbled, likely telling him shit he didn't care to know. Just when I believed I was getting through to him, Shark gripped my forearm and dragged me to a nearby chair at one of the five cheap wooden tables in the small dining area.

He shoved me into the torn red leather bottom of a wobbly metal chair. I landed hard enough that I was forced to grip the edge of the table to keep from tumbling to the floor as the chair grunted angrily beneath me.

"How the fuck did you know I was Shark?"

I'd asked around, questioning people like a detective, and tipping them money for anything I could find out. I even spotted a few of the August Knights rolling around town that I'd followed like a shadowy stalker. No one was the wiser that I wanted anything to do with these people outside of my curiosity and therefore my snooping didn't raise any red flags.

I pointed my shaky finger at Shark's chest. The black leather vest he wore was filled with his MC's patches. The word, "President" was on a patch that stuck out on his chest. Anyone who knew of the August Knights Motorcycle Club around this area knew that Shark was the president. Although he looked meaner than a rattlesnake about to strike, he stopped looming over my shaking frame and took the seat across the table from me.

"Talk," he spat the single word in my direction.

The background silence was as alarming as Shark's presence. The hum of the AC unit and cursing drunks outside were the only sounds that carried over my thundering heart. Without glancing at them, I sensed the hot gazes of the group inside boring holes into me from every direction.

After relaying my reason for being there to Shark twice more, the tightness around his eyes remained, and his piercing glare of uncertainty increased in its intensity.

"So, let me get this shit straight." He cut me off in the middle of one of my shaky sentences about helping my sister.

"You drove out here to n*gg*r-lynching territory to broker a deal with me so that my men would leave your drug-addicted sister alone?"

I flinched at the sound of the N-word being voiced so loudly in public. Truth was, I was one woman in the middle of redneck alley. Therefore, there wasn't shit I could do or say about him using the N-word.

I nodded, answering his question. The oddest thing I'd seen since I arrived happened next. Shark began to laugh, releasing a deep boisterous chuckle. His shoulders shook and he tapped at the table like I'd given the ultimate punchline.

The tension in my shoulders coiled tighter as Shark's roaring laughter spread throughout the room. Although they had no idea what he was laughing about, others began to laugh with him.

There was no doubt in my mind that Shark thought I was a damn fool, and he was probably right. I knew as well as the next person that this was about as insane a move as I could have made. However, I had to convince them that I was determined to do everything in my power to save my sister.

CHAPTER TWO

Megan

After a stressful half hour of being interrogated by Shark, I believed he finally began to understand my position. The contents of my purse were dumped all over the table before my shirt was yanked up, exposing my bra, in search of a wire. The three men he sent to search my car returned, shaking their heads to indicate they'd not found anything suspicious.

It took a lot more of me repeating my story before Shark became convinced that I wasn't law enforcement. His sharp expression told me he wasn't fully convinced, but his posture was less hostile after calling to check out my story about my sister.

"I don't have much money to give you, so I can work for you as a bartender, a dishwasher, or even a maid," I said, glancing around the room.

"As long as it's not illegal, I'll work off my sister's debt."

It was likely naïve thinking on my part, but I didn't fear this group having a desire to sleep with me or even rape me. I was sure they would have preferred to die rather than bed a *black* woman. But it didn't mean that they wouldn't hurt me in other ways or worse, kill me.

Shark waved a few of his men over to the table. Three stood on one side of him and two on the other, all staring at me like I was the new chew toy they all wanted to see if they could break.

"Men, I need your input. This...*woman* has made me an interesting proposal with respect to squaring a debt her sister owes us. Option one, which is I can allow her to work for us until the debt is paid in full. Option two, send her back from where she came from because we don't need the extra headache."

"Those are the only options?" one man asked, his face squinted, his gaze flashing his disdain for me. The same contempt was present in the rest of their expressions. The men weren't keen on the idea of me working for their MC.

"Those are the only options," Shark finally answered.

"I say we toss her in the nearest river while she's barely breathing," one suggested.

"That sounds like the best option," another agreed.

One couldn't resist adding, "I'm tired of looking at her black face already. Shark, are you really thinking about entertaining this crazy shit? You're going to let her work for you? For *us*?"

Shark didn't answer the man. Instead, he pointed out, "This is the craziest shit I've ever encountered, but even you must admit it takes nuts the size of Texas for someone like this to find me and risk her life to make a proposal to square someone else's debt. Now, I don't associate with blacks and neither does anyone else in this room, but if you find one who stumbles into your place and pretty much offers to be your slave to square a debt..."

He shook his head in disbelief with a wide grin spread across his face, his eyes sharp as blades and aimed at me. "I don't see how you turn some shit like that down. And, this bitch isn't all the way crazy."

Shark raised the two business cards I handed him during his interrogation.

"She was smart enough to let a few detectives know that she was coming to see us. Told them she was a writer who wanted to interview us for literary integrity or some shit. The pigs advised her against it but couldn't stop her from doing what she wanted on her own free *stupid* will."

Shark shook his head, I suppose to shake off my crazy plan before he proceeded.

"I say we put this bitch to work. See how it goes for a few days and if she works out, we let her work off her sister's debt and not on her fucking back either. There's no fucking way I'm authorizing any of you to have sex with a black woman. There is enough cleaning, bartending, and stocking she can do. A month's time should square her sister's three-thousand-dollar debt."

A few shrugged, but none of the men voiced an opinion. A couple of irritated grunts sounded, and a few heads nodded uncaringly. One stared at my face with wide unblinking eyes like I was a unicorn.

Shark continued, his gaze slicing through me. "Long as she stays the fuck out of my way and does what she's told, I say let the bitch clean up after us. What's the worst that can happen?"

The grumbles from the men increased. Shark slammed his fist on the table, making me jump. When a few of the men stepped away, I concluded that the impromptu meeting was over.

Shark aimed a stiff finger at me, "Honey, you have officially sold yourself into slavery for thirty days. I hope that sister of yours is worth it because it's going to be a bumpy ride."

The slick grin he flashed unnerved me as snickers sounded around the table. His deliberate use of the N-word and the word, *slave*, rattled my nerves and sent fear coursing through my veins.

"Think we should get a rope or better yet a whip?" one of the men asked Shark with a low, throaty whisper. They continued to stand around the table while I remained glued to the seat I'd been slung into, unsure of what to do with myself.

Shark stood and slammed his fist down on the table again making the wood vibrate.

"Didn't I just fucking say she was clever enough to let the authorities know that she was coming here? Anything fucked up happens to her, this is the first place they're going to look. We don't need the fucking pigs sniffing around our door over this stupid bitch. We'll let her work off her sister's debt, and that's it. As much as I would like to have a good old-fashioned modern-day lynching, it's not going to happen…at least not with *her*."

Shark's mean scowl intensified as his voice deepened. "Do I need to repeat the part about not fucking her? From what I hear, black pussy makes white men do strange shit."

A long pause followed the insulting comment. He wanted to make sure his words were understood. A round of head nods and grumbles sounded. This man was seriously fucked up about race, but he was the devil I was willing to deal with.

Was grunting and grumbling all these men knew how to do? Why had Shark felt the need to reiterate to them that they were not to fuck me? I assumed they found the idea of sleeping with an African American woman repulsive.

"Jake, since you or your brother was stupid enough to give her sister drugs on credit, you take her to drop off that rental she drove up in and pick up whatever girl shit she might need for thirty days. We can't have her coming and going around these parts. There are too many damn rednecks around here. We don't need them nosing in our business and we definitely don't want one of them to get her."

Copper County, Florida, was the area in which I had foolishly driven myself. The area was known for its racial divide. Since the county was eighty percent Caucasian, based on a few reports I'd read, their warped view of race remained unchecked.

Jake screwed up his clean-shaven baby face, gripped his shoulder-length hair and sighed heavily, upset about having to babysit me. Shark pointed a long authoritative finger at him, the mean glint in his gaze daring Jake to test him further.

"Straighten out your fucking face, take her to drop off that car, and come…right…back."

Shark's daring eyes raked over the group once more before the music and low murmurs resumed. The decision was final.

"I'm tired of talking about this shit. It's giving me a fucking-ass ulcer. Are we done with this, so we can talk about real business?" Shark asked the few remaining men standing around him although I was sure he didn't want to hear any responses.

A series of low grumbles sounded after Shark's statement, but no one was bold enough to challenge or question him. My gaze darted around the table. This was it. I'd gotten in. Now, all I had to do was survive the next thirty days amongst a racist MC of dishonest, venomous, and coiled rattlesnakes.

Before I could think my way through what had just happened, Shark's tall, bulky body was in front of me again. His hand was big enough to wrap damn near around my entire shoulder. He jerked me from the chair and shoved me toward the front door.

"Go and get rid of that car, get your girly shit and baggage, and come right back. I'm putting you in the spare bedroom in the back. Once you come back and put your shit away, I want you to start working on the kitchen. It could use a good cleaning."

Since my voice was stuck, I nodded and skirted my eyes away from his. As I shuffled toward the front door, I snuck a glance back at the kitchen which was visible from my location through two open double doors. If the boxes stacked from floor to ceiling and the dirty countertops littered with dishes were any indication, it was likely going to take the full thirty days to get the kitchen cleaned.

Jake's face pinched into a noticeable pout. He picked up where his president left off, shoving me the rest of the way to the front door.

I stumbled out of the door; thankful I was no longer the main attraction. Shit, maybe I was. The tethered white blinds in the dusty windows that I would be cleaning later were being pulled apart in various spots as I took hurried steps toward my rental.

They peeked, stared, pointed, and ogled me like I was an escaped animal. I sensed their hateful gazes boring into me, but I was not equipped to do anything but endure the hatred and complete the task I'd set out to do.

I climbed into my rental, and the good sense I had left urged me to leave this place and never come back. Good sense always seeped from my fractured brain before I got the chance to use it. But I couldn't abandon my task, not after I'd gotten myself through what I believed was the most fearful part of this situation.

CHAPTER THREE

Megan

A few hours of sleep was all I could manage through the night. I was stuffed inside the tight, smelly space of the broom closet posing as my room for the next thirty days.

There were no alarms or wake up calls, just the loud shouts of men and their heavy steps beating against the creaky floorboards. I cleaned and kept my distance by hanging out in the kitchen, but my resolve was being vigorously tested.

It was only the second day, and the weariness of my situation was settling in. I'd worked through my fears and gotten this far, therefore, my determination to see this thing through would remain my main source of strength.

The mission of some members of this motorcycle club was to seek me out and see how many times they could push me or call me the N-word before I broke. Whenever I encountered them, they taunted me with demeaning words, shoved me, or demanded I work faster or harder. They enjoyed that they could say the N-word in front of an actual African American and get away with it without being challenged.

Numerous times, I caught Shark staring. He made no attempt to hide the gleaming lust in his eyes. Was it possible to hate someone and be sexually attracted to them at the same time?

I was a curvy five-foot-five, brown-skin woman with lengthy, curly hair. I was not a glamor girl or a magazine beauty, but over the years, I paid attention to what men specifically liked about me, and I have not been afraid to use those features to my advantage when necessary.

Although I'd been blessed with full lips and big, brown eyes shaded by thick lashes, I was aware that my ass was known to get me noticed faster than my other features.

I didn't have an insanely large ass, but mine wasn't small either. It was round and plump enough to attract attention. My chest barely made its way into a C-cup, but my slim waist made my chest appear larger than its actual size.

Currently, my ass poked out from me being bent over the sink scrubbing the hell out of a large stainless-steel pot. I glanced over my shoulder while Shark approached me. His eyes danced in their sockets before zooming in on my ass.

I turned around to avoid giving him a target to concentrate on and his gaze dropped to my tits. Never mind the big, baggy T-shirt and sweatpants I wore. His fixed eyes looked like he saw right through them.

He'd forbidden his men from touching me, and now I wondered if it was because he wanted to sample me first. He didn't say anything, but stopped, stared, and walked away, like there was nothing at all strange about his behavior.

I proceeded to carry on with my business. It had taken me most of the afternoon to wash the dishes and clean the large stove and refrigerator. Grease and dirt were caked on the stove, and the refrigerator was teeming with mold and food items that had taken on new life forms. Whoever cooked for the club wasn't the most sanitary person.

Since no one bothered to offer me lunch or any kind of food, I made an executive decision and prepared a meal. I opened a few cans of mixed veggies, made gravy from scratch, and used the passable beef cubes I'd found in the large freezer to make a beef stew.

Shark didn't object when he noticed me cooking, and despite how messy and dirty the large refrigerator had been, it had been well stocked.

After dusting off and washing the rice cooker, I steamed a pot of rice to go with the stew. I doubted I'd have any takers, but the food would be there if the group wanted any. If they didn't, I would have something to eat for the next few days.

When Shark walked into the kitchen and found me sitting at the small, splintered table in the corner eating a bowl of stew, he didn't hesitate to pick up a plate and dig in himself. I stared so hard at him; I dropped my spoon.

My eyes crinkled at the sight of him eating my food. How did he know he could trust me not to poison him?

It took Shark a few minutes after he exited the kitchen through the swinging double doors to return for a second helping. The next thing I knew, other members of the MC came into the kitchen in groups of twos and threes, following Shark's lead.

They stood around the pot like hungry vultures. The members of August Knights Motorcycle Club were a group who weren't supposed to trust or like me, but they sure as hell didn't seem to mind eating my cooking.

It was strange that there weren't any women that hung out in this club. Did they come at a certain time? Was this club for men only?

Based on what I was seeing, this group needed to re-think their no-women-allowed policy because they didn't seem to come across many home cooked meals. It didn't take long for them to scrape the pot of stew clean. Maybe cooking could be a way for me to get on their good side—as good a side as they had that would allow me to get through these thirty days unscathed.

I stared absently through the window while washing the last of the dishes I dirtied. The worn, puke-green blinds in the wide kitchen window presented a stripped view of nothing but woods.

The sun was setting, diming the daylight, but it didn't take the heat with it. The old AC unit sitting below those ugly green blinds may as well have been a fan. All it did was swirl the heat around the kitchen and leave me drenched in sweat. The rusty decorative thermometer tacked to the wall near the window showed an inside temperature of eighty-four degrees.

Although muffled by the closed kitchen doors, a rowdy string of shouts drew my attention and spiked my heart rate. It sounded like someone yelled out, *"Drop the gun, motherfucker!"* but I couldn't be sure. Loud outbursts weren't unusual among this group.

***

I stepped cautiously into the small hallway that led to the club area, stopped and tilted my ear up to listen. Dead silence answered back. Had I imagined what sounded like trouble brewing?

My gaze landed on the closed door on the opposite end of the hall as the double doors that led into the club. Earlier today, I snuck into the room and learned that it was the club's conference room or whatever bikers called their meeting area.

I pushed the door open and stepped inside, wanting more than just a peek this time. A large hardwood table filled most of the space, which had a biker and motorcycle carved atop the surface in such intricate detail it drew my attention.

I stared at the table like one would a piece of art in a gallery. Ten heavy black leather rolling chairs surrounded the large table. A wooden gavel that matched the table's surface sat at the head, Shark's spot.

The walls bore chipped white paint and nails stuck out at various angles where members hung their vest, I presumed. Sheer and dingy pale blue drapes hung in three large windows that framed the wall running the length of the table. No other items or furnishings were in the room.

Another round of loud shouting drew my attention back to the club area. It wasn't so much the shouting, but the intensity of it that gave off a vibe that made the atmosphere swarm with tension.

I crept toward the swinging double doors and listened, placing my ear to the wood. Using my shoulder, I cracked one door open, and a violent string of curse words assaulted my ears. Before I could figure out what was happening among the throng of angry men, all hell broke loose. I didn't run from the drama, I eased the door open further and stepped over the threshold for a better view.

If I was going to be stuck with these bikers for another twenty-nine days, I figured I may as well get some enjoyment out of it. Fist and elbows. Curse words and shuffling feet. A group of about six were beating the hell out of each other as bystanders got caught in the crosshairs of the fight. A few of the guys I recognized from Shark's group tussled with men who I assumed were from a rival MC, based on their cut.

Bikers were beating the shit out of each other, and I was enjoying the show, my gaze dancing over the scene with keen interest. Angry punches landed and beer bottles were cracked across necks as non-fighters scrambled for cover.

My head swiveled back and forth, left and right, as the clatter of pounding fists, angry shouts, and growling barks exploded throughout the club.

When a gun came skidding in my direction and clinked to a stop at my feet, I stared at the shiny piece of black metal before I reached down and picked it up. It was an FNP45 caliber pistol, which confirmed that someone intended to kill someone. I learned about guns from my dearly departed husband who died fighting in Iraq three years ago when his unit was ambushed by Iraqi forces.

I identified the gunslinger as the dirty, stringy-haired blond on the receiving end of Shark's fist. Shark had knocked the gun from the man's hand after he'd raised it to Shark's face, intending to kill him.

Bam! Bam! Bam!

I jumped at the sound of each shot fired. The loud series of gun blasts made all activity cease. Fists froze mid-punch, wide-eyed glares darted from every direction, and heaving bodies remained in place.

Pieces of the ceiling tile crumbled to the floor like dusty rain from the impact of bullets. The same stringy-haired blond who lost his first weapon to me must have had a backup and hadn't hesitated to open fire inside the club.

"I came here to broker a deal with you." He aimed a stiff finger at Shark. "Now, I'm going to blow some fucking brains out and be done with it. You wild animals don't know nothing but violence."

Although the man was talking to Shark, his weapon was trained on another one of Shark's men. Thoroughly confused, I continued to watch the scene unfold. If his intent was to kill Shark, why would this man come to Shark's club with only a few men? Were there others from his crew outside? Had these men come willingly, to go out in a blaze of glory? Was this the biker's way?

One thing was for sure, at least a few of the questions firing off like rockets in my head were about to get answered. Shark's glare was so menacing it chilled me.

"Did you think you could sneak in here with three men, snuff me out, and not be dealt with?" Shark asked the man. "I hope you have backup coming, Scud, because you're about out of time."

Shark took a step closer despite the man's gun remaining aimed at the head of another August Knight.

"If I had a gun in my hand, you would be dead, and this meaningless conversation wouldn't be taking place." Shark spit out the words, anger riding every syllable as he crept closer to the gun wielder.

The man known as Scud tightened his grip on his gun, maintaining a steady aim. "Keep talking, Shark, and I'll splatter your brother's brains all over this dirty-ass floor."

The man snickered at Shark. He knew his actions would hurt Shark more if he killed his brother in front of him. He also had the most power in the room because he was the only one with a gun.

The scene baffled me. I was under the impression that bikers of this sort were always packing. However, I do recall hearing something about guns not being allowed in the clubhouse.

From what I could gather, the three men with the purple shirts under their vests knew or had found out about the no-gun rule and had made a fool-hearted attempt to sneak into the clubhouse to cut a deal or assassinate Shark. I didn't know what their true intent was, but they hadn't put together a well-thought-out plan.

Scud, the would-be assassin, yelled his request at Shark, "Release my men or watch your brother die."

One of Scud's men's face's kissed broken glass atop the bar as he was being held down by two August Knights. Scud's other man was uselessly attempting to squirm his way out of a strong chokehold being applied by an August Knight who was a descendant of giants.

Shark shook his head, letting Scud know he had no intention of letting his men go. The next ten seconds happened in a blur. The metallic click of Scud's weapon drew every eye in the room. Shark's brother shut his eyes under the weight of impending death.

There was only one person in the room who wasn't looking at Scud. Shark glanced at me instead. His gaze going to the gun hanging forgotten in my hand. When his sharp eyes locked with mine, he inclined his head once. I honestly don't know how I knew what he wanted, but I did. Shark wanted me to lift this weapon and shoot Scud.

On one hand, I couldn't kill a man in cold blood, especially since I didn't know the full story of why or how he and Shark's crew had gotten to this point. On the other hand, shooting this man could possibly win me favor with the MC.

Bam!

The oily scent of gun smoke made my nostrils flare just as the man in my sights went flying back. The height of the bar hid Scud's fallen body from my view. I aimed for his shoulder and prayed the whole time I didn't hit him in the chest. I didn't want to kill him, but I didn't feel bad about shooting him either. I was surrounded by criminals, so it wasn't like I'd shot an innocent victim.

I know, my damn mind was twisted, a fucked-up freeway of illogical ideas. But, in my defense, the man had come and threatened to kill Shark who was technically my boss. An August Knight near the fallen Scud raised the second weapon Scud lost during the fall.

As my conscience sought to make an appearance, Scud's bloody hand gripped the counter. He lugged his body up before staggering forward, clutching his shoulder. His loud grunts didn't garner any sympathy from this crowd.

Shark's gaze met mine before he raised his splayed fingers. I tossed him the weapon still warm from the shot I'd fired. I was in such a state of astonishment that none of my actions were registering. It was like I was on autopilot. Had I really just shot a man for an MC that I'd only worked a day and a half for?

As soon as the weapon hit Shark's hand, he didn't hesitate to use it.

Bam! Bam!

Scud went down in a dramatic display of sharp jerks and twitches. Based on the spray of blood from his head and the hole Shark had put in his chest, Scud wasn't getting back up this time. Shark tossed the weapon to his brother, the one who Scud was holding at gunpoint.

"Take them out back," Shark commanded. The finality and authority in his voice weren't lost on me.

I observed and filled in the blanks. Taking the men in the purple shirts *out back* must have meant taking them out to execute them.

Scud's men were forced out of the front door by August Knights. Without being told, one of Shark's men hoisted Scud up under his limp arms, dragged his lifeless body, and followed the group to wherever *out back* led.

I stood in place, not moving, until I glanced into Shark's pleased face. I'd been so busy watching the scene unfold that I hadn't noticed that Shark had inched his way into my personal space.

"You did good," he complimented. "Are we going to have a problem with you keeping any of what you just witnessed to yourself?"

His firm stance and set jaw explained what his words couldn't. He was asking if I would rat them out. I'd shot someone at his command, and it wasn't enough to convince him that I was as crazy as they were?

To keep from becoming the next one sent *out back*, I swallowed my sudden emergence of annoyance. "I've seen much worse growing up. You have nothing to worry about. I didn't see shit."

After those words, I turned away from Shark to return to the kitchen. There was no need for him to tell me what I needed to do. Although I didn't understand all of their rules, common sense gave me insight on how this world worked. I filled a bucket with warm bleach water, grabbed the mop, and gathered some old rags.

Without being told to do so, I went back into the club area. The room had thinned considerably. The twenty or so bikers who eye-witnessed a murder were outside, likely witnessing two additional executions.

The men who remained stared at me approaching the crime scene with the cleaning supplies. Why the hell were they staring at me when they sent a body and two men *out back*? I was nothing but the cleaning lady.

Shark eyed me as I strolled past them and stopped at the bloodstained floor. It pleased me that I didn't see any brain matter or chunks of human tissue.

Shark approached. Again, a pleased smile danced across his face. "This isn't your first rodeo, is it?" he asked.

Was it surprise or pride I saw flash across his face and disappear just as quickly? Was my behavior intriguing to him?

I shook my head before I began my task of cleaning up the blood and what I assumed was urine that Scud had released when he was struck with the lethal shots. I sensed Shark standing behind me, staring until one of his men called him away.

CHAPTER FOUR

Megan

As I entered the second week in the craziest deal of my life, I noticed that my actions in shooting Scud had earned me only a marginal amount of respect from the MC. I earned just enough that the bikers no longer wanted to drop me into the river. And, luckily for me, Shark stood between me and any impending dangers where his MC was concerned.

Although I did a fairly good job of staying out of the Shark's way, I still faced my fair share of difficulties. I endured two heated groping sessions where I was cornered and discovered that race had nothing to do with sexual appetite. If it weren't for Shark's authority and stringent rules regarding not fucking me, I would have ended up experiencing what it was like to sleep with multiple dirty bikers.

Thankfully, for me, Shark spent most of his time at the clubhouse where I slept, cleaned, and cooked. I'd also been tasked to clean the MC's bar, which was about seven miles closer to Copper Springs, the small town right off the main highway.

The bar was like the clubhouse, except it was bigger and was stocked with a larger amount of alcohol. Women were allowed at the bar. The only time I was allowed away from the clubhouse to clean other areas was during none-operating hours.

I didn't know shit about bartending but used the best-guess method of mixing their drinks when they asked. A few flashed me funny looks or frowned while swallowing what I gave them, but none voiced any complaints. This let me know that they didn't care what they were drinking as long as they were getting drunk.

I listened for any piece of useful information and picked up enough clues to learn the MC had a hand in selling guns and drugs. The clubhouse I slept in was mainly a hangout spot exclusively for the members as well as the meeting place or 'church' as they called it for members and the club's chairman.

Shark wanted me at the clubhouse because it kept me hidden from the public. I didn't mind it because exposure to the public in Copper County was just as bad if not worse than being tied to the August Knights.

Most of the men continued to treat me like an outsider, but the longer I stuck around, the more they allowed me to see and hear information about the inner workings and operations of their club.

The MC labeled the women as "old ladies" or "property" and didn't hesitate to trade unclaimed women if it was what suited their needs. The women claimed as personal property belonged to one member. Guns and drugs were their main source of income, and the few businesses they owned I believed were meant to clean their illegal money. Only family members were made chairmen, and the MC recruited only Caucasian men.

Motorcycles, the things I expected to see most, weren't as prevalent as I assumed they would be. Most of the men drove huge pick-up trucks and biked occasionally or socially on planned bike rallies and group drives.

I was getting the inside track on the way a real motorcycle club lived and considered it one of the perks of my new gig since I was actually a writer. After days of enduring their name calling, grabbing, and shoving, the men all but forgot about me until they faced me or needed me to do a chore.

It was human nature to adjust to certain ways and behaviors, and I was starting to adjust to these people who considered me their enemy. It got to the point where I was hearing the N-word less. I wasn't a head doctor, but I would venture to say that even the racists got tired of being racist after it no longer fascinated them.

* * *

By the end of the second week, I'd graduated from the N-word pincushion to the dejected bastard child. The MC's old ladies or property weren't going to accept me or adjust to me as quickly as the men. When I was asked to clean the bar, the women taunted me worse than the men ever did.

When at the clubhouse, my temporary home, I cleaned whatever I needed and kept to myself in the broom closet of a room Shark had assigned me. I slept in a twin bed that had a mattress that was no more than a lump of moving rocks. Therefore, I was thankful I'd bought a sleeping bag on the one chance I'd had to go to The Mart, their version of Wal-Mart.

The mattress I slept on stunk like the MC had been stashing dead bodies inside it. I had washed the bedding several times, and it continued to exude a vile odor of stale dick droppings and ass juice. I slept tucked snugly inside my sleeping bag, no matter how hot it became inside the tight room with its tiny window.

The scent of weed occasionally floated into the small air vent above my bed and thankfully, kept me just high enough to keep the funk from invading my soul. There was no way I was sleeping on the pillow that was obviously stuffed with dirty drawers. I used my backpack as a pillow.

Fortunately, I'd brought my laptop and was grateful they allowed me to keep it. Since writing was my only escape from the situation in which I'd thrust myself, I continued to write and market my work.

My thirty-day stint with the MC had come as a surprise, one Shark had drawn out of thin air. However, I noticed something I had neglected to think about the first time I faced him. No one would miss me if I never went back home. The two detective's business cards I had given Shark were fakes I printed myself. It was a little insurance that I believed would keep the MC from killing me on the spot and dumping me *out back.*

These bikers had no idea that I was a severely damaged woman who occasionally ventured outside of societal norms. They were clueless that I'd sat and planned how I would approach this MC for months before I decided to act. Shark was right about his initial assessment of me. I was crazy. Possibly insane. My mind was twisted, but I'd learned to hide it well.

CHAPTER FIVE

Aaron

Our Motorcycle Club's dangerous reputation and its history of violent crimes, arrests, and murders had earned us a certain level of respect that was required in our line of business. It had also left a spotlight shining on us; not only by the authorities, but it also cast rival eyes in our direction. Over the years, my father and I had discussed ideas and implemented plans that were designed to take the spotlight off us.

Hard work and planning kept most of our activities hidden. It had taken time, but my father and the rest of the MC acknowledged that whispers about our reputation were just as effective if not more so than broadcasting our aggressive actions for all to see.

My father had made his own feeble attempts, but I remained the MC's go-to guy for finding conventional ways of doing business without calling too much attention to ourselves. After I'd returned from the military over three years ago, my father suggested I do most of the planning, although I earned money for the MC running guns. My cousins handled the drugs and my uncles the strip club, which included managing the women.

Based on the worn appearances of the strippers, we would be wise to burn the strip club down with the women inside and start over from scratch, but it wasn't my call.

It was my suggestion that we implement more business-like practices that would at least make our MC appear legit and offset the expensive tastes and habits certain members had adopted. The bar, the car washes, and several coin laundries had been purchased over the years to clean our dirty money. The businesses also provided legitimate jobs to members whose criminal pasts prevented them from finding employment anywhere else.

I maintained a steady job as head of security for the local town of Copper Springs' largest security firm, Fox-Butler. As a result, many of the men in the MC worked under me. We posed as full-time or part-time security officers, which served as cover jobs to help offset the outlandish lifestyles some of us were determined to live.

Sometimes, I wondered what life would be like outside my MC, but this was the life I was born into and all I knew. Besides, I'd participated in so many illegal and lawless activities that I believed I was too far gone to be anything other than a gunrunner and enforcer for my MC.

Outside my stint in the military, I never sought a way out of this life. It was an interesting parallel that the life I grew up in had prepared me for the military, and in return, the military had armed me with the knowledge and skills that made me a force to be reckoned with when I returned to my world.

However, just because I had embraced this life, it didn't mean I liked it all the damn time. I was grumpy more often than cool, went from zero to asshole in a heartbeat, and spoke my mind, good, bad, or ugly. A few of the older MC members said I had a black heart, but my heart wasn't black. It merely sat farther back in my chest than other peoples' hearts did as far as I was concerned.

My father had me cutting coke by the time I was seven and cooking meth by the time I was ten. My mother, who was thankfully dead, had put her fist in my face every chance she got. I had witnessed so many murders; many of them at my own hands, that I was becoming numb to the gruesome nature of It.

I took the lives of many. Some in self-defense, others for crimes against my MC, and a few to prove myself as Shark's son.

The safe inside my secluded house in the woods contained over two hundred thousand in cash and my offshore account contained five times as much. The kicker was I didn't know of shit I wanted to spend that kind of money on. Other than motorcycles and the occasional woman who caught my eyes, there wasn't much else that piqued my interest.

After shoving the familiar doors of our clubhouse open, I heaved a quick breath before entering. I hated this fucking place and having to go to church. Why couldn't I show up once a month, say my piece, and leave? My father made me an MC chairman, so I was required to attend.

In my opinion, we were nothing but a bunch of ruthless rednecks who hated as easily as we breathed; mainly because we couldn't stand our own fucking reflections. Many of us were so hateful and deceitful that it seemed our mission in life was to make everyone around us miserable.

I combed my fingers through my hair, gripping my scalp for a second while entering the boardroom. A heavy duffle bag was clenched over my shoulder as I headed for my spot at the table. My boots beat up the floor, blending in with the noise of the crowd stuffed into this room.

The large spoke-wheeled motorcycle and rider carved into the table caught my eyes, and I concentrated on it to keep myself grounded. My younger brother, Ryan, had sketched the carving. Ryan was the artist in the family. He was designing and inking tattoos before he'd hit double digits. However, our dangerous lifestyle had snuffed out his life before he became a teen.

The men sitting around the table were already yelling across the space at each other, undoubtedly, about shit that didn't matter. Grudgingly, I lugged myself over to my chair next to my father who sat at the head of the table. The stench of cigarettes and the scent of leather introduced itself before I took my seat.

All eyes landed on me when I heaved the big black duffle bag full of money and guns off my shoulder and handed it to my father. The bag contained three-hundred thousand dollars and a variety of guns the group had asked for. I was like the criminal version of Santa Claus to this bunch of ungrateful assholes.

Years prior, during my four-year tour as a marine, I'd brokered a deal with the son of a German gun supplier I'd met. The deal with the new supplier allowed us to run guns much faster than our original Russian supplier. The Russian supplier had refused to let us out of the on-going deal my father had brokered before I was set to take over gun operations.

Long story short, one of the first tasks I took on after I completed my tour in the military was to kill our Russian supplier before we took on the new deal.

Now, we purchased guns at a discounted rate, and sold them to the Mexicans at a rate below market value that they agreed to. In turn, the Mexicans supplied us with quality cocaine, and we distributed it to several trusted distributors, including our gun supplier. These transactions occurred monthly with the occasional special request.

For my trouble and coordination, I roughly profited a half a million or more a year, give or take a few hundred thousand.

My father handled the process of sharing the wealth with the MC's other chairmen, the grumbling assholes I currently sat and stared at with disdain. Hopefully, the disdain reflected in my gaze was strong enough to blind each of those bastards in one eye. You only needed one good eye to do the half-ass jobs they did anyway.

Every guy at the table had a specific job, and my father thought himself a stickler for job performance, although goals were rarely met, and tasks were never completed to standard in my opinion. It could have been the military coming out of me, but I believed in detail and order.

During the course of the meeting, my gaze was drawn from the issue we were addressing, because I swore I saw a black woman…a good-looking one, walking toward me.

I closed my eyes and attempted to shake off the fatigue that continued to plague me from my trip. I hadn't slept in twenty-four hours and still had tasks I needed to complete before I headed home.

Shit! I must be tired as fuck.

When the woman walked around the table and started setting dishes of food down in front of each chairman, my weary gaze tracked her every move. No one was saying a goddamn thing to explain to me; one, how a black woman was roaming freely throughout our clubhouse and two, why the hell she was serving us food.

My penetrating gaze cut into my father's, who was shaking his head and attempting to do everything in his power to keep from bursting his gut with laughter.

"It's a long-ass story, son. I'll tell you after the meeting's over," he informed, acknowledging my bemused expression.

"Would you like something to eat, sir?" The delicate voice barely made its way into my ear.

Am I awake right now? I asked myself the question as I watched members at the table eating whatever it was the woman had served them.

I glanced at the woman still standing next to me. I assumed she hadn't moved because she was waiting for my answer.

"No, thank you. Not hungry."

My elbows hit the table, and my face fell into my hands as I massaged my head. When I glanced back up, the woman had moved on to my father.

Good God. The woman was gorgeous, and despite being brown, her presence was eye-catching. I scratched

my head, realizing this was the first time I had noticed…truly noticed a woman of color. Since I was
forbidden from being around them all my life, my reaction
to my attraction to this one was justified, I supposed.

When she offered my father one of the bowls of food
she had on the tray, my gaze zoomed in on the dish. My
father leaned away and allowed the woman to set one of
the bowls in front of him before he expertly took up the
napkin and spoon she'd set in place and began eating.

Soon after the exchange, my father continued his conversation like I wasn't sitting there, freaking the fuck out
at what was happening. Were their lives in jeopardy and
they, for unknown reasons, couldn't say what was happening?

I placed my hand on the .45 tucked in the back of my
pants. Weapons weren't *supposed* to be allowed in the
clubhouse, but I was the enforcer, so I was never without
a weapon.

The crease in my face deepened, and the veins below
the surface of my skin started to pound. My gaze left my
father and followed the woman, who was heading back
into the kitchen.

She wore a long-sleeve, baby blue, cotton T-shirt and
thin cotton sweatpants that were about two sizes too big,
although it was July and hot as fuck outside.

My eyes swept around the table as spoons clinked
against bowls and rose to their working mouths. Lips
smacked, and even a few grunts of satisfaction escaped.
Was anyone planning to tell me what the fuck was going
on? My chair creaked under my shifting weight as I sat
higher and leaned over the table.

The weight of my frustration was expressed in my voice. "Does anyone plan to tell me what the fuck is going on? Are my eyes fucked up or did I just see a black woman inside our clubhouse boardroom serving food that all of you, crazy motherfuckers are eating?"

Throats cleared and wide gazes traveled toward my father. So, my gaze shifted in that direction too.

"Son, she's working off a debt for her crack-head sister. Your dumb-ass cousins let her drug-addicted sister get away with about three grand in coke, and *this one* was crazy and brave enough to come out here and work off the debt to keep us from killing her sister."

My gaze traveled around the table. This shit just wasn't sinking in.

"If you ask me, she is just as fucked up as her sister for doing suicidal shit like this. So far, she hasn't been any trouble, so we've agreed to let her work off the debt. The only law I laid down concerning her was that no one was to fuck her. I can't allow any of you to get tangled up in some black pussy. Now, if you need your house cleaned or a maid, she's a good cleaning lady and a pretty good cook." My father tossed one of his hands in the air. "Look around, son. Haven't you noticed we've done some remodeling?"

Stunned, I just sat there, searching for words as I gave the place a once over. When I'd walked in, I was so concerned about getting the meeting over with that I hadn't even glanced too far past my own damn feet.

"Are you all fucking crazy?" I asked, my wide gaze scanned the room. "What if she's the law and you're in here freely discussing business around her? Not to mention the fact that you just let me walk in here with money and guns. What if she has a team of fucking lawmen waiting on some line for one of you to say the right thing that will take all of us down?"

"Son, calm the fuck down," my father said as he leaned toward me. "What do I look like? A fucking fool? I checked her out and had her checked out again. I know how to spot a fucking rat. I've been in this business longer than you've been alive. If I believed she were a danger to us, she would be buried with the rest of the bodies. She writes books—one of them nerdy bitches. Her books and shit are all over the internet, and that crack bitch of a sister of hers is in rehab just like she told us she would be. I gave her a month to work off her sister's debt. The only place we could keep the public from seeing her is in this clubhouse."

What the fuck? For my father to do something this reckless, he must be losing his damn mind. Shark glanced around at the other chairmen, who nodded, agreeing with him like always.

"Like I said, she hasn't given us any trouble. She even helped us get rid of some vermin, Nelson Cates' son, Scud. Fucker came in here after sniffing his balls, thinking he was taking me out. Shit, I'm thinking about keeping her ass for good. She shot that bastard and kept him from blowing Wade's fucking brains out."

Wade nodded in my direction, confirming my father's words. I was so fucking confused that my head began to ache. The veins in my forehead pulsed under my skin, threatening to pop out and spray my tired blood all over the table. It took my father's last words a moment to take root inside my brain.

"She shot someone? Tell me you didn't just say she shot someone. What the fuck is going on around here?"

Grinding my fingers into my temples, I roughly massaged my forehead. I was only gone a few weeks. How could our world have changed this fucking much?

"Son, relax. I'll give you the full-court press when this meeting is over."

On cue, the pretty woman stepped back into the room with cups and a pitcher of something to drink.

Instead of listening to the rest of the shit my father was spewing, I was too busy attempting to figure out what alternate universe I had landed in.

"Would you like something to drink, sir?"

Sir?

This was the weirdest situation I believe I ever experienced. I caught a glimpse of the woman's bruised arm when she attempted to hand me one of the cheap plastic cups. Those bruises reminded me of the hellish world I grew up in, and I couldn't imagine the shit my MC had likely put this woman through.

"No, thank you," I finally answered her without looking back this time. My gaze landed on my father, my anger flaring. "Speaking of cousins. Jake and Jackson fucked up again," I uttered. The words erupted from my mouth through gritted teeth. I waited until our new maid went back into the kitchen before I continued.

"I don't know if he and his brother are taking the drugs they're supposed to be selling, but I had to pay Dixon the two grand he claimed they shorted him. I went ahead and paid him to keep things cool, but I'm going to need you to get my money from them. If I face them, I'm going to whip their dumb redneck asses."

Shark nodded, aware that I would make good on the promise. Much of the rest of our meeting went the same, with us discussing the problems we faced while attempting to stay on a straighter path than the deviant, body-dropping one we couldn't seem to shake.

***

By the time my father got around to telling me the full story on our new maid, I had already pieced most of it together. My father was right. This Megan was one crazy bitch. She had purposefully subjected herself to a bunch of bikers known as racist for the sake of saving her sister.

From what I surmised; her sister wasn't worth a damn. Megan managed to infiltrate my MC, and it was a stunt that I wouldn't have been bold enough to attempt. There was something Shark wasn't telling me. There must be more to this than what he was saying.

"Why don't you take our little maid for a few days?" he suggested, making me snap my head up so fast it caused a sharp pinch in the side of my neck.

"Let her give your place a good cleaning. You can use her work as a small down payment on the money Jake owes you."

I stared, flashing him a have-you-lost-your-fucking-mind look.

"Fuck no! You want me to bring her into my house. Just because she has you fooled that she's some crazy bitch trying to save her sister, it doesn't mean I'm going to jump on the bandwagon and believe that shit too."

"Son, you were the one who suggested we become more *mainstream* and look more legit. We can't get any more mainstream than this. Since it's so damn late, I'll drop her off at your place tomorrow."

I didn't feel up to arguing with him. Occasionally, he made questionable decisions. Was he coming down with signs of early dementia?

My grandfather had developed the brain sickness when he was in his fifties, and my father had just turned fifty-two. I had already decided, if I started forgetting long stretches of time, I was eating a fucking bullet or two if the first one didn't work.

I squinted at him to gauge his mental state before releasing an irritated sigh.

"Whatever. I'm going to take care of a few more drops and take my tired ass home. I don't have time for this kind of crazy shit you have going on here."

I stood and walked away with not so much as a glance back. I had fucking seen and heard enough for one day.

CHAPTER SIX

Aaron

The blaring sound of a horn caused me to tumble from my couch. The first thing I picked up was my gun, shoving it down the waistband of my pants. I crept to my window, peeled back my white curtains, and peeked out into my front yard.

I had purposely built my house in the middle of woods so that the only way to access it was by a dirt road that required a truck to navigate it. The trail was so rutted, I couldn't even ride my motorcycles along it. I rode them through the woods or was forced to truck them out to the clubhouse if I wanted to ride.

My house and the land I built it on had all been purchased under a fake name. If my enemies were to ever show up at my door, I knew two things: they meant business and they were there to kill my ass.

After I left the clubhouse last night, I made a few more business-related stops and hadn't made it home until after 9 o'clock this morning. I blinked and rubbed my eyes to knock the sleep from them before glancing at my watch. It was 5:30 p.m. I had popped an Ambien, and until that damn horn sounded, had slept like a log.

After dropping my curtains, I clumped toward my front door, sprung it open, and stepped onto my wraparound porch of my two-story log-style cottage.

My hands automatically clenched when I saw who was walking in step behind my father. I forgot all about his crazy-ass proposal that I take the woman as a down payment for the money my cousins owed me.

I was sure my father noticed the cold indignation on my face as I watched the woman trailing him and simultaneously shot missiles at him with my glare. I pictured his ass getting blown to kingdom come repeatedly.

The woman had a purple backpack slung across her shoulder, and her gaze remained on the ground. I couldn't help the deep crease in my forehead, but any protest on my part at this point was grounds for an argument with my father, and I didn't want the fucking headache.

Without speaking, he walked past me and shoved my front door open. He waved the woman in before he entered and left me standing on the porch like he was the fucking owner of *my* house.

Before making myself go back into the house, I mouthed, "Fuck. Fuck. Fuck."

"Wait in the kitchen while I talk to my son, Mona," my father said as he pointed the woman toward my kitchen. I could have sworn he said the woman was named Megan.

"Son, no fucking her. Keep your dick to yourself. I know you damn young people and the way you're wired. You don't care about mixing up the gene pools, and I'll be damned if any son of mine or even kin of mine get themselves tangled up with some black pussy. God forbid, I end up with a mixed-up grandbaby. Jesus!"

He shook his head and winced like the idea was unholy.

"I'll be back to get her in a few days—three or four. Put her ass to work."

He waved his hand absently around while glancing around in my living room. "From the looks of this dusty-ass place, you could use her."

With those words, he walked his feeble-minded ass out, not giving a damn about anything I had to say. I knew my father better than he thought I did. If his only rule was for me not to fuck the new maid, it meant that he had likely been tempted. His reverse psychology didn't work on me like it worked on the rest of the MC.

***

I walked into my kitchen and found Megan already working. *Well shit.* Maybe my father was right about this crazy woman wanting to keep her sister alive.

She stopped scrubbing one of my plates and glanced back at me when I walked further into my kitchen. I eyed her before making a head gesture toward the back stairs. "Let me show you to your room."

"Yes, sir."

My hand shot up as I shook my head in protest. "You can stop with that sir, shit. I'm not my father. I'm not deep into that old-school racist shit either. If you respect me, I'll respect you. Just don't piss me off and you'll have nothing to worry about."

"Okay," she said in a quiet voice before picking up her backpack.

She followed me, as quiet as a church mouse, up my back stairs. Was this seriously the same woman my father claimed had shot Scud?

I twisted the knob and shoved the door to my spare bedroom open. Standing in place, I waved her in. She and her backpack squeezed past me. Based on the expression on her face, she expected my place to be a dump. However, I possessed more standards than anyone would give me credit for based on who I associated with.

"Clean whatever you think needs it. Cook whatever the hell you can make from the kitchen. Make a list of the groceries and shit you think you might need, and I'll pick them up tomorrow. Long as you stay out of my way, we won't have any problems."

"Okay," she said, her tone low and unassuming.

"Do you say anything more than "Yes, sir" and "okay?" I asked.

"Yes, but I was told to shut the fuck up and be the maid, so that's what I've been doing."

I can see why that would limit her vocabulary.

"Did my father fuck you? Did any of the other MC members fuck you? Have you been beaten or harmed in any way?"

I was about as mean a motherfucker as you could encounter, but I didn't believe in harming women or children unless it couldn't be avoided.

After my question, I saw her swallow from across the room. I was rough, harsh even, and that included the way

I talked. I came across as a mean bastard and preferred it that way.

"Your father announced that no one was to fuck the n*gg*r. Two members tried after they got me alone, but after I threatened to tell him, they left me alone. Other than a few grabs, shoves, and pushes, no one has beaten or harmed me."

My eyebrow lifted, but there was nothing more I could think to say in such an odd situation, so I just walked away.

CHAPTER SEVEN

Megan

Sweet relief filled me when Aaron walked away. I blew out the breath I was holding, and air finally flooded my lungs. Aaron was one of the most intense men I'd come across in a long time.

For as scary as Shark was, his son was much more intimidating. Shark was tall and beefy, and although he had a huge scar on his face, he wasn't bad looking for a man more than twice my age of twenty-four.

Aaron, on the other hand, was muscular, and his strong medium frame belonged in a magazine. He was at least six-two or three and weighed over two-hundred pounds. He was tall enough that he didn't look bulky like The Hulk, but his muscles were defined and rippled under his clothes.

There was no way you could *not* notice him. He was one of those good-looking men who'd been drenched in pure sex appeal. Not classically handsome, but attractive in an edgy and tousled kind of way. It didn't matter what he wore—you'd only be interested in the man beneath the clothes. His every movement seemed measured and confident, and he had the bad-boy biker attitude to go with it.

Unlike his father's dark hair, Aaron's dark-blond tresses reached his shoulders. His slightly darker brows sat above intense light blue eyes. His eyes were such a piercing shade of blue that he had the ability to hypnotize you if you stared at him too long.

His kissable lips were a deep shade of pink and sat above a manly beard the same darker tint as his brows. The unkempt beard somehow worked in his favor and brought a spark of excitement to what otherwise might have been considered too pretty a face for a man.

I was supposed to be unpacking or cleaning, but my twisted mind wanted to linger on how unbelievably sexy the man was. Aaron's body was pure sin. There was no other way to describe it.

Unlike his body, the clothes he wore were ugly; well-worn dark jeans, a black biker's vest covered with what must have been every club patch they'd named, and a holey black T-shirt underneath. On his feet were black combat-style boots that confirmed he had a big-ass foot—at least a size thirteen.

'You know what they say about men with big feet?' Popped into my warped mind. Why was I this fucking crazy? The places my mind traveled to sometimes—I swore crazy was being injected into my brain with a needle.

Despite his good looks and how pretty his blue eyes were, Aaron's gaze was so menacing, it chilled me down to the bones. There was a storm raging behind those eyes, just waiting to be set free to destroy whatever it touched. His presence unnerved me and made me fidgety and unsure about every move I made and every word I said. He would go down as one of the most intensely scary people I'd encountered in a while. So, why the hell did it excite me?

In the short time that I was in his presence, I sensed the blood on Aaron's hands. The intensity in his eyes had initiated a story that he didn't have to tell out loud. The glass-cutting edge to his voice conveyed pieces of his history as well.

Despite him being a redneck and a dangerous biker, Aaron had a beautiful home. When Shark drove off the main paved road and headed down a series of bumpy, tree-lined dirt roads, my heart nearly leaped from my chest, thinking he was taking me somewhere to kill my ass, like *out back*.

When he'd driven up to and walked me up to the huge log cottage, I grew more surprised than scared. When Aaron opened the door, I dropped my gaze and bit into my lip to keep my damn mouth closed.

Like now, I stared around the spare bedroom he led me into that appeared to have been professionally decorated. The country theme wasn't my taste, but even I had to admit the space was beautiful and something to appreciate, especially after the room his father had given me to sleep in at the club. I may as well have spent two weeks sleeping inside the rotting carcass of an elephant.

The queen size mahogany bed in this bedroom sat against the main wall built to look like long logs. The bed was adorned with a blue and brown flannel patterned comforter and four large fluffy pillows. It sat between two large windows that promised a view of the woods through its open flannel pattern curtains that matched the comforter. A nightstand and two large dressers made of beautiful teak stood at different heights and finished filling the room.

When I walked into the bathroom, I found the open-face wooden wardrobe stocked with fresh towels, most of which still had tags on them. There was soap in bars and liquid and even lotion. The amount of dust that had settled over the place indicated that Mr. Intensely Scary and Good Looking didn't entertain often.

I believed I would have a more difficult time trying to keep from staring at Aaron than I would have cleaning his place.

CHAPTER EIGHT

Aaron

The sound of pots banging, and the aroma of food told me that my guest was in the kitchen cooking. I had no idea what the hell she was cooking, but it smelled good as fuck.

I had fallen asleep on the couch as I did most nights, and the rousing of my guest had awakened me. The sun hung dimly in the sky, and the low hums of different insects let me know that it was early morning. My ass had passed out and slept all night.

After I'd shown Megan to her room, I headed back to the couch. My intention was to finish watching a basketball game I started, but sleep had dragged me under and kept me down.

Not used to having another living soul roaming around in my house, I had instinctively reached for the pistol I kept in the shoulder of my couch. Come to think of it, I may have to put away the other guns hidden throughout the house. However, my guest's intentions were validated by the fact that I was still breathing. She'd had all night to plot and plan my murder if it was her aim.

I forced myself to sit up so I could take a piss. As I leaned forward to stand, my guest stepped into the living room, carrying a plate piled high with food and a glass of something to drink.

She greeted me with a forced smile as she handed over the plate that I gladly took since my fucking stomach was eating my insides alive. I was sure I was missing a small intestine.

"Good morning, sir. I meant, good morning."

"Aaron. You can call me Aaron and thank you," I said, annoyed that she kept calling me sir.

I believed it surprised her to hear me thank her. Considering she'd been under the care of my father and the bunch of goons he was determined to raise in his image, I could understand her reaction.

"You're welcome," she voiced in a low tone.

She pointed at the glass in her hand of what I now noticed was water.

"There was only water and beer. I brought you water unless you'd like a beer."

I reached for the sweating glass of ice water, and my fingers inadvertently brushed her hand. Her skin was so damn warm and soft it didn't even feel human. I cleared my throat and brushed away my reaction.

"Water is fine. Did you make a list of shit you think you may need? I'll go and pick it up later today. It doesn't matter what you put on the list, I'll eat just about anything."

That includes your pussy, if you'll let me.

Down, boy. My ass needed to get laid before my fucking balls turned three shades of blue. And little Miss Mouse was looking about as tasty as a fucking piece of freshly baked apple pie. She was an attractive woman. I couldn't deny that truth.

She lowered her head, thankfully unaware of what I was thinking.

"Yes, I made the list already," she said, before turning and dashing back toward the kitchen. She was running from me like I was a fucking monster. I shrugged. I didn't blame her because I was. I was a scary-looking mother-fucker. I knew as much, but most women liked that shit.

After sniffing at one of my armpits, I wrinkled my nose. My ass was musty and dusty from my trip. I didn't just smell like yesterday, I stunk like hot garbage, but a shower would have to wait because I intended to inhale the plate of food I was given.

The fluffy scrambled eggs still had steam flowing from them, and the ham had been seared to perfection. The two fat, fluffy biscuits had butter drizzling over their golden-brown tops. The first few mouthfuls caused my eyes to close with appreciation.

"Damn, this shit is good," I mumbled under my breath.

Now, I understood why the MC hadn't turned down the food she'd set in front of them the other night. Megan could have poisoned the whole damn upper echelon of my MC if she'd wanted to. But, that sly band of hoodlums was still very much alive.

She'd managed to survive with them for two weeks without permanent damage, which meant that she'd earned a certain level of trust from them whether she knew it or not. Maybe she was as resourceful as my father had claimed and as crazy as I knew she must be for agreeing to do some shit like work for my MC.

I wolfed down the huge plate of food in minutes and gulped my water while shuffling toward the kitchen. The scent of cleaning products hit my nose before I reached the door. When I swung it open and stepped into my kitchen, I stalled.

The scene before me made my mouth drop open. I could literally eat off the damn floor. My kitchen was cleaner than it had been the day I walked into the finished house three years ago.

The sounds of shuffling and humming drew my attention, but I didn't see my houseguest. I peeked around several corners before I walked over my dishes and sat them in the sink.

When I walked past my kitchen island, I found Megan on her hands and knees. Half her body was in the pantry and the other half was bent over and sticking outside the door. Her ass was on full display, and despite the oversized clothes she wore, it was easy to see she had a nice one.

Leaning farther over for a better view, I discovered she wore earphones. Although I couldn't see the device they were attached to, the purple earphones in her ears had her head tilting left and right as she sprayed Pledge and dusted the lower shelves of my pantry.

My fingers cupped my chin, musing over the details my father had revealed about her. He wasn't lying about her being a worker, that's for damn sure. I glanced around my kitchen once more. To have it looking this clean, she had to have been working since daybreak.

My shoulders lifted in a quick shrug, and I smiled. Maybe this wasn't a bad idea after all. When I turned to head back to the living room, the list of shit I'd asked her to make was sitting on the counter.

"Well damn."

The woman didn't waste time, that's for sure. Now, I further understood why the damn clubhouse and bar appeared to have been remodeled. All they needed was a good cleaning, and based on my kitchen, the new maid didn't mind doing a thorough job. That sister she claimed to be helping must have been all she had left in this world.

***

Sunday was the only day I didn't do a damn thing but watch sports, lounge, and drink beer. After a long hot shower, I headed back to my couch.

It seemed like minutes, but it must have been hours. When I opened my eyes to the beautiful face staring down at me, I froze, thinking I must have been hung up in a dream.

Brown was not a color I associated with pretty things, but her big eyes were the prettiest shade I'd seen in a long time. They weren't a light brown but more like a burning orange and brown mixture that sat like big adorable perfectly placed orbs of light. Those lush, full lips were a brownish pink that blended perfectly with her bronzed, unblemished skin.

Megan's perfectly arched brows went from slightly arched to extremely when she changed her facial expression. Even her nose was cute. It was too late for me to pretend like I hadn't been staring. I made her uneasy enough to cease all movement.

Although common sense told me that most of what I learned or had been taught about blacks wasn't true, I believed I was about to discover that more of the shit didn't have an ounce of truth to it.

I liked Megan's cooking *a lot*, but more than that, I liked *her*. I was as attracted to her as I would have been to any other woman that caught my eye. I fought the effects of where my mind wanted to linger.

"I brought you lunch if you're hungry," she said after I stopped ogling her and glanced at the plate in her hand.

I hadn't woken enough for me to decide if I was hungry or not, but I wasn't going to turn down what I believed were chicken and dumplings. Breakfast and lunch on the same day. I had hit the fucking lottery.

There wasn't a time in my life that I could remember getting a home-cooked breakfast and lunch on the same day. If she kept cooking like this, I didn't need to put off going shopping. How did she manage to scrape together two complete meals from my kitchen?

"Thank you," I told her, fighting to keep from staring. I was sure she hadn't missed the way my lingering gaze stalked her body.

"You're welcome," she replied.

Just as she had that morning, she hurried back to the kitchen, taking quick and quiet steps.

The curves of her body played out in my head until the flavorful aroma of the food lured me back to reality.

I ate, enjoying every mouthwatering spoonful before my attention was returned to her. If Megan's aim was to poison me, I prayed the shit killed me fast.

Why did it seem like she was running from me? Why did it bother me? Each of our encounters were uncomfortable and brief like we were avoiding something.

Was I scary enough to cause her to run? Maybe I was staring too hard. My tattoos, the long biker hair, and the beard I was thinking of chopping off—it may have been too much for someone as innocent-looking as her.

This time, when I entered the kitchen, I spotted Megan in the pantry stacking my canned goods. The clinking of my plate and glass as I placed them in the sink had her peeking out of the doorway.

She wasn't plugged into her music this time. Her phone sat on the countertop. The low buzz of a familiar tune spilled from the headphones and drew my interest in her taste in music.

Quick steps led me to the pantry where I purposely invaded her personal space by standing in the doorway. With no place to run from me this time, she didn't have a choice but to back away from me.

"Are you afraid of me?" I asked, realizing with that question, my sharp tone was likely intimidating.

She dropped her gaze and lowered her head, but I wasn't sure it was fear I was reading in her subtle movement. I'd scared many motherfuckers, but something was telling me that it wasn't all fear I saw in Megan's facial expression.

"You don't have to be afraid of me," I assured her, taking a little of the bass out of my voice.

I stepped into the pantry and invaded her space further. I liked seeing her squirm against my approach as I continued to inch closer, keeping my gaze on hers until I had her pinned to the back wall of my pantry.

"Humph," she grunted when her back hit the wall.

My anxious hands lifted, and I pressed them against the wall on each side of her head while her gaze stayed on my chest.

"Megan, look at me," I demanded.

She did, and I'd be damned if she wasn't one of the most beautiful women I'd ever laid eyes on. A sprinkling of cute brown freckles dotted her nose and cheeks and could only be seen this close up. The urge to kiss her sprang up in me before I could figure out where it had come from. My eyes dropped to her lush, tempting lips, which enticed me to lick my own.

My head dipped, falling close enough to hers to draw in her warmth. My hungry lips were inches away from hers now. She held my gaze, searching for my purpose as her warm breath brushed over my face. I sensed how good it would feel to close the last few inches separating us so that I could feel her lips on mine, against mine, and between mine.

"I'm not going to hurt you" I said, before a stray idea crossed my mind. I was unable to keep the telling smile from twisting my lips. "I won't unless you *want* me to."

She continued searching my eyes without responding as her breaths came in fits and starts, the only sound bouncing around the tight space of my pantry. Despite her nonverbal response, she drew me in more. Words I'd intended to keep in my head started pouring from my lips.

"I don't give two fucks about what my father said. If you ask me to or gave me permission to, I'll fuck you any way you want."

Her lips parted, but she didn't or maybe she *couldn't* speak. The visible tremble of her body was turning me on so badly that a stream of blood shot to my dick. It was as hard as the lead pipes on my chopper. My gaze swept over her lips and the quivering pulse in her neck before roving back up to her wide eyes.

I desperately wanted to give myself over to the pull toward her. As I observed her reaction to my closeness, I was certain that I wasn't the only one swimming in sexual tension

Just when I made a move to back away from her, I spotted what she'd attempted to keep hidden from me: lust and desire. A combination of the two was shadowed by her fear. She was afraid of me, but a part of her wanted me too.

I stepped the fuck away from this woman before I ended up doing something I had no business doing. We'd barely spoken complete sentences to each other, but I couldn't deny the unspoken chemistry swimming around us. If she asked me to fuck her right now, I wasn't sure I'd be able to resist the request or my urges.

CHAPTER NINE

Aaron

"Megan!" I shouted for her because I was ready to go shopping before I drank another beer and passed the hell out. We were supposed to go shopping yesterday, but after our pantry episode, I kept my distance before my dick led me down a path I wasn't supposed to take.

Quick steps brought her into the living room, and she didn't stop until she was standing timidly before me. "Yes."

"Are you ready to go so we can get the things on the list?"

"You want me to go with you?" she asked with her brows lifted high.

"Yeah. Is something wrong with that?"

She shrugged. "You're not afraid of being seen with me?"

My face scrunched with confusion. "Why the hell would I be afraid of being seen with you?"

"When I rode with Jake, he made me climb into the back bed of his truck and duck down. He said he didn't want to be seen with a n*gg*r."

I didn't know what to say to her. Some members of my family didn't understand that most of the world didn't give two fucks about their racist views.

"My cousin is a fucking idiot. Do whatever you need to do. Fix your hair, straighten your clothes, or whatever it is females do before you go to the store. Then, grab the list so we can go."

My words sounded clipped, but it usually didn't take people but a day or two to realize that it was just my way.

Megan returned a few minutes later with the list in her hand. Aside from making her high ponytail neater, she looked the same. She had on a pair of those pale blue, designer-looking sweatpants, an oversized, beige T-shirt that seemed not to want to cover one of her flawless brown shoulders, and black and white Nike tennis shoes.

I think she intended the outfit to hide that ridiculously seductive body of hers, but no amount of extra material could hide what my eyes were trained to see. She was the equivalent of a living, breathing representation of pure temptation. All I could do was see how much longer I could resist it.

***

Once we stepped into The Mart, I began to understand what my stupid cousin was getting at about not being seen with Megan. I noticed the funny looks right away, but other than that, people kept their opinions to themselves. They fucking well better had, if I had anything to say about it.

To avoid me cursing someone out, I suggested, "Hey, maybe we should split up. You work on that list, and I'll grab the things I need from the automotive section. Make sure you get what you need and whatever else you think we need for the house."

I hadn't missed that she'd almost smiled at me, but she suppressed it and kept a straight face. "I'll meet you at the registers?" she asked.

I gave her a quick nod before turning and stepping away. I could have helped her with the list, but I hated shopping and hated the way people's eyes followed our every move. I was doing what was best to keep from cursing a motherfucker out for eyeballing us. The strong silent type—he was not me. I was the quick-tempered type, and there was only so much I could take before I lost my patience.

After taking a few steps away from Megan, two mean-looking black men approached me. Their expressions warned me to prepare for a fight, but their sudden smiles met me before my anger took over. One of the men reached out his fist in a gesture for me to give him a fist-bump. I bumped my fist with the man's but questioned why he'd initiated this friendly gesture toward me. My questioning gaze met the man's.

"You a lucky man, bro. She's *nice*."

My eyes followed theirs to Megan and the reason for their friendly gesture toward me. They must have seen me with her and automatically assumed she was my woman. She was unaware of what was happening as she read the label on an item in her hand.

I didn't correct the men's assumptions. Instead, I took their compliment and prepared to move the fuck on. "Thank you. Appreciate it."

The men walked away shaking their heads like they had shared something I didn't already know. If there was one thing I knew, it was that Megan was definitely *nice* as they'd put it. She had no idea I had random men complimenting me because they believed she was my woman.

I rounded the automotive aisle and scanned for the wiper blades I needed for my truck. As my fingers grazed over blade after blade, searching for the model and size for my truck, male voices on the other side of the aisle confirmed that the conversation about Megan and me wasn't over yet. The two brothers who'd approached me earlier were loud and unaware that I lurked near enough to hear them.

"Did you see what that white boy strolled in here with? Lil' Momma was fine as fuck. A dime for sure."

"Naw, brah, she's one of them women who will break the scale. She a dime with sweats on, so imagine how fucking fine she is when she's fixed herself up. White boy got him a platinum piece."

My smile widened at their conversation. Was this how men viewed women? I leaned my ear closer when they continued their colorful conversation.

"I bet white boy catches hell from niggas mean mugging his ass over her. I was ready to give him shit, but after I saw her, I was like, nah, let me give this cracka his props for choosing wisely and shit."

The men laughed loudly. One cut through the laughter and added, "Man, she one of them women you'd kill a motherfucker over. Somebody look at her the wrong way, and you'll be ready to whip a nigga's ass or shoot a motherfucker."

I bit into my bottom lip to stifle a grin. Now, I didn't feel so bad for being attracted to Megan or for losing my shit when I was close to her. She affected men who'd never even talked to her, and here I was sharing a house with her.

After finding the blades I needed, I picked up air fresheners for my truck and headed toward the registers. The sight of Megan waiting for me enticed me to smile for no reason. The half-filled basket of goods sat next to her as she thumbed through a magazine.

"Ready?"

She jumped at the sound of my voice.

"You got everything on that list?"

She took a quick glance into the basket. "Yes."

"Okay, let's go," I said, tilting my head toward the nearest register. I placed my hands on the bar of the basket before she could and wheeled it toward the shortest line.

Judging by the way her mouth had dropped open, she didn't expect me to help her unload the groceries onto the conveyor belt or load them into the bed of my truck.

I'll admit, I'm fucked up in certain areas of my life, can even be an asshole at times, but I'd never been one to abuse a woman, not even the poor white trash that danced at our club or hung around my MC's bar all the time.

Therefore, I saw no reason to treat Megan any differently because her skin was darker than mine or because of the warped rules my MC believed they needed to follow. Besides, I decided from the moment I laid eyes her that I was not only attracted but would also fuck her if the opportunity ever presented itself.

CHAPTER TEN

Aaron

Later that evening, I informed Megan that I wanted to eat dinner at my dining table. When she sat my food in front of me and attempted to run away, my hand clamped around her wrist to keep her in place. I caught a hold of her rougher than I intended to, but my action stopped her in her fast-moving tracks.

My eyes remained on my hand wrapped around her warm, soft wrist. "I want you to join me. I want to hear the story from your mouth…the one of how you landed this so-called maid's job with my MC. We've had fucking deep cover agents that couldn't have done what you're doing right now."

Once I released her wrist, she dashed off to fix her plate. She returned to the table and took the seat across from me. I listened to her story intently as she updated me on her sister's drug use and her constant struggle to save her from herself.

The military taught me what to look for in body language to spot lies, and Megan, as far as I could tell, was genuine in the telling of her story. The flow of her tense words and the strain of sorrow she failed to cover when she talked about her sister were indicators. However, if

Megan was telling me the truth, it wasn't the whole truth. There were more than a few sentences missing, she was leaving out complete chapters.

It fascinated me to find out that she truly was an author. Her making a living from writing was impressive. This was a new endeavor for me, to have a genuine interest in someone other than a target or potential business associate. I was interested in Megan. Previously, my interest in women had never gone past me fucking them.

When Megan handed me her phone, I paused. My gaze pivoted between her and the phone before I reached for it. She'd pulled up multiple online sites that sold her books, and to my surprise, there were many. The information made me that much more curious about this woman.

Her story caused me to question the negative shit that had been drilled in my head about blacks my entire life. Megan didn't fit into any of the stereotypes. The more I talked to her, the more I was convinced that lies had been shoved down my throat from the start. Thankfully, common sense made me acknowledge as much, and I realized it was possible that everything I'd been taught could have been a bunch of lies and stereotypical bullshit.

Interested in more aspects of her life, I swiped through her cell.

"What kind of music do you listen to, Megan?" I asked as I searched through more than music. I wanted to know about the things she wanted to keep hidden. The damn chapters she'd skipped over when telling her story.

She reached for her phone. Once she had it, she swiped and tapped the screen a few times and handed it back to me. "This is my master playlist. I listen to everything."

Lifting an eyebrow, I tapped the screen and hit shuffle. The first song that popped up was a country tune that I enjoyed by Florida Georgia Line. While the song played, I glanced at her, eyeing her with suspicion. I listened to about a minute of the song before I shuffled to the next one. A classic rock tune by Journey played, followed by a heavy metal song. A rap song trailed that song, and a few other different genres of music followed.

"You thought because I'm African American that I only listen to rap and R&B, right?"

It was exactly what the hell I'd thought. I couldn't lie.

"Yes. That's what I thought. As a matter of fact, a lot of what I was taught doesn't seem to be true, not for *you* anyway."

The ice had been broken, and her tension eased enough for her to talk more openly now. A tiny crease lined her forehead.

"Unfortunately, a small percentage usually represents the whole of us in society's eyes, and it's usually the worst of us that the spotlight gets shined on," she said.

I understood exactly what she meant. The media always found the biggest, meanest, and most illiterate redneck around and presented him or her to the world as representation of all of us.

I let the music play until one of my favorite country tunes by Garth Brooks spilled from the speakers. My feet tapped under the table as my mood lightened even more. My eyes skimmed over the delicate features of Megan's beautiful face before landing on that silky brown shoulder that peeked from the top edge of her shirt and gave a glimpse of what she tried to hide.

Although she didn't appear old enough to be a widow, she shared that her husband was a soldier who was killed in Iraq three years ago.

As a former marine, I understood deployments and military life. I'd nearly had my head blown off in Iraq and was damn near blown to hell in Afghanistan. I still had a few pieces of shrapnel in my back as a result of my time served.

After her husband's death, Megan claimed she'd turned into a recluse and poured her heart into her fiction writing. The writing paid off and turned into a livable income. Other than her sister, she had no family. When she was younger, the state had dumped her into and yanked her out of six foster homes by the time she was twelve.

The glints of sorrow in her droopy eyes when she spoke of foster care indicated the hard time she endured while in the system. However, she did express more emotion talking about foster care than she had talking about her sister. Seeing her attempt to swallow the emotion she fought to keep off her face sparked a need within me that made me want to do something to take that look off her beautiful face.

Wait! Where the hell was all this coming from and more importantly, how was she making me feel this way? I changed the subject before more unusual shit decided to creep into my brain.

"So, you spent all of your savings getting your sister into a top-notch rehab facility? Then, you turned around and did something as crazy as pawn yourself off to a bunch of dangerous bikers like us, all so that you can clear up the mess that she made? Have you considered that we could still end up raping or killing you?"

I leaned over the table, my eyes sharp and I'm sure intense.

"Just because you shot someone in front of my MC doesn't mean you're safe. We are not good people. We have lots of enemies gunning for us, and you could get caught in the crosshairs of our turmoil."

Her facial expression never changed as she contemplated my words. There was alarming intrigue in her expression, something I wasn't expecting to see. My comments should have been frightening to her, but I don't believe they were. There was something peculiar about this woman that intrigued me as much as it alarmed me. Was she naïve, stupid, or manipulative?

"You do realize that any number of things can happen to you just by hanging around with our kind? We have been attempting to refine our behavior and the way we conduct business, but we are still very dangerous people."

I squinted while staring at her, speaking my words with purpose so that she would understand what she had truly gotten herself into by dealing with the August Knights. Aside from the steady flow of her breaths, those big brown eyes with their long, flirting lashes were all that moved as she considered my words and observed me with a curious glint.

I was so aware of her that I could literally see her dark pupils swell each time her gaze landed on my lips. She was checking me out as much as I was checking her out, studying me just as I was her.

No matter how fascinating Megan was turning out to be, something was strangely off about her. I talked of raping and killing her, and she hadn't even flinched. Something wasn't adding up, and I couldn't put my finger on what was off about her.

"I think there is a lot more you're not telling me, Megan. For you to do *this*, something this extreme, tells me you're not as afraid of this environment or any of us as you'd like us to believe. I think you're insane or you're probably one of those women who gets off on being scared."

Something I couldn't identify sparked in her eyes at my statement. I'd always been a good puzzle solver. Megan had jagged parts and pieces that were never meant to be put back together. Hints of darkness peeked out from the veneer of innocence she presented.

People took in my appearance and assumed I was a dumb redneck biker, but I'd always been more inclined to learn and plan before I acted. As a result, I became a good problem solver and business negotiator. I also become a predatory killer, one of my MC's most dangerous weapons. Being this way made me patient; patient enough to piece together a good puzzle, even one as complex as Megan.

"I am going to download one of your books," I blurted.

A smile.

I'd finally managed to put a smile on her beautiful face. Straight white teeth flashed in front of me and made her face even prettier than before. I twisted my lips to keep from returning the smile.

There was nothing that I noticed that I didn't like about Megan. I liked that she didn't have to wear fancy clothes or spend hours on hair and makeup to look beautiful. Nature had taken care of everything where her beauty was concerned. Although she worked constantly, she always managed to look clean and give off a fresh scent, but not perfume-fresh. It was more like she kept fresh showers in her pocket.

My gaze fell to the small diamond studs in her earlobes and then moved to those long, flirty lashes that introduced the seduction hidden behind her eyelids that I wasn't sure she was aware was there. The lushness of her full lips lured my eyes to her mouth. I paused there before allowing my gaze to drag over her neck, which was not lost or sunken into her shoulders.

Her neck was long enough for me to wrap my hand around comfortably to control several positions I wouldn't have minded putting her in. The fluffy and bouncy texture of her curly dark hair was as flirty as those damn lashes.

My lips twitched at the roundness of her tits. By my eye's measurements, they would fit perfectly into the palms of my hands. The tempting curve of her ass, that I'd eyeballed multiple times, was surely capable of taking a good pounding from the back. My eyes hadn't missed that ass, not even the first time I'd seen her at the clubhouse.

Although I hadn't seen her naked, I pieced together enough to know that her body was toned and sexy as fuck like she spent her free time working out when she wasn't working for dangerous bikers.

She was sitting there watching me virtually undress her with my eyes. Unlike before, she didn't seem bothered by it now. Her gaze followed my finger when I pointed at what I believed was a small scar on her arm, higher near her shoulder.

"What are those marks on your arm?" I asked, dropping my hand on the table to stop myself from reaching over to touch her.

"It's a birth control device," she said, glancing down at the spot.

"That's good. Smart. That way, if one of us raped you, you wouldn't have to worry about getting pregnant."

Megan lifted her gaze from mine but didn't comment. I stared at her for a solid minute, attempting to fill in the blanks of what she wasn't telling me. My unflinching gaze finally made her fidget, and I don't think it was because she was scared. She picked at the food left on her plate, avoiding my eyes now.

She was hiding something, and I wanted to know what it was. I wasn't going to stop until I figured her out. She was on my radar now, and I didn't know if it was a good or a bad thing for Megan.

Unable to take my staring, she stood, gathered the rest of the dishes, and proceeded to wash them by hand despite my owning a dishwasher. I remained at the table with a smile spread across my face. My beast was stirring, and he wanted to devour Megan in every way imaginable.

***

The light drum of my fingers against the table sounded as I scrutinized Megan and half listened to the music spilling from her phone. She'd finished the dishes, but to avoid me, she began wiping the countertops down, rubbing so hard she was about to take chunks of the granite with each swipe.

Standing, I intended to leave. All I had to do was step away from the table and head to the living room, but she just kept drawing me in and the pull was so hard, I couldn't leave. Instead, I crept up behind Megan and invaded her personal space as she continued to pour her energy into that countertop.

Her hand stopped moving the instant she realized I was close. She didn't turn in my direction when I placed my hands on the counter on either side of her warm body and locked her in place. My nose sat above her curly ponytail, and I sniffed loud enough for the sound to carry.

My nostrils flared, taking in the soft fruity scent she emitted. Her hair smelled of freshly plucked peaches. I dipped my nose closer to her neck and found that her skin smelled of chocolate covered strawberries. The soft, flowing scents mingled as they invaded my senses and caused me to close my eyes to savor them longer and deeper.

Her accelerated breathing over the low tunes I left playing on her phone in the background added a depth to my already heightened arousal. I inched closer and didn't stop until my hard dick was pressed into the soft curve of her ass. She gasped at my invasion but didn't push me away.

I sank into her soft flowing curves. With my chest pressed into her heaving body, I placed my lips to her ear. "You're out here in the middle of the woods alone with me. There is no one that can help you for miles around.

No one can hear you if you scream. What would you do if I fucked you right now?"

Her breathing kicked up a notch, and I liked it. No, I *loved* it. The pulse in her neck jumped, straining to keep her heart from exploding, and I didn't know if it was fear or arousal that caused her to react this way.

Her body heaved up and down against mine. Breath after noisy breath brought a spark of life to my kitchen that the music couldn't, but she didn't say a word. The movement of her body, however involuntary, made my dick harder, so hard, in fact, it ached. My lips brushed the tip of her earlobe, causing her to shiver.

"What would you do, Megan? Because I'm not going to lie to you. I want to fuck you right now."

She turned around, rubbing her warmth against mine. The tremble in her limbs revealed that I was scaring the shit out of her. Despite her obvious fright, she managed to glance up at me. Her words were low and shaky, but she had the courage to speak them.

"There's not a thing I could do. It doesn't matter that no one can hear me because no one around here would help me even if they did hear me screaming."

My hands had grown heavy with an ache I never felt in them before now. I peeled them from the counter, fighting not to do what I knew I shouldn't—*touch her*. If I touched her right now, there was no telling what kind of rules I would break.

The ache in my palms spread, and I couldn't resist gliding my hand up her side. My thumb ended up scraping across the hard tip of Megan's nipple. The action made her breath hitch. Her eyes fluttered closed, but she recovered quickly and reconnected her gaze to mine.

She was afraid of me, but at the same time, my touch turned her on. I could tell by the way her lips fell apart and how hard her nipples were, as I continued the feathery flicks of my thumb across one.

Megan was giving it a good effort, but she couldn't hide the flaming heat blazing in her gaze or the lust that hung heavily in her eyes. Seeing her react to me only heightened my arousal and reminded me that I hadn't been with a woman in a lot of fucking months. The realization, the touching, the scents, the heat, it all made my breathing kick up a few notches, and Megan's reaction was feeding my insatiable need to lose complete control.

I couldn't fucking fight it much longer. One second, I was testing her to see if it was lust or fear she was hiding. The next second I lifted her onto the countertop and drew her roughly into me, spreading her legs around me. She dropped her gaze and heaved deep breaths as her arms were forced to rest at my sides.

One of my hands gripped her ass, holding her against me while the other one roamed her body taking liberties, I didn't have permission to take. Her hand that sat shakily against my abs began to creep up like she was unsure of what to do with it.

Her other hand had a tight grip of my shirt on the opposite side. She was displaying the same behavior that caused me to act this way in the first place. On one hand, she was terrified while on the other, she'd taken a hold of me.

I pressed my bearded cheek against hers, enjoying her soft warmth as it radiated into me. My lust-filled whispers kissed her ear.

"I want to fuck you, Megan. I want to fuck you so fucking bad that I can hardly stand it. Fuck, you're killing me."

Lust had turned me into a raging monster. But I had to regain control and calm myself because Megan obviously had no idea what she was doing to me. I needed to pull it together. Plus...*rubbers.*

I'd never brought a woman to my house, so I was sure I didn't have any fucking rubbers. Megan had made no attempt to fight me, so I lingered.

"Can I fuck you with no condom, Megan?"

This question got her attention, and for the first time, she eased her head away from mine before she scooted away from me. She released my shirt, and her trembling fingers were no longer massaging my abs. Her gaze captured mine.

"I hope that you won't, but there is not much I can do about it if you force it."

The word *force* dialed down my intensity. She may as well have poured a bucket of ice over my head. I never had to force myself on any woman since most freely offered me their pussy.

"I don't have anything," I informed her; unsure of why I felt the need to share the information with her.

Megan had me talking crazy and ready to do crazy shit. At twenty-seven, she had me ready to break a major rule I had set for myself and had followed emphatically over the years. The last time I fucked with no condom on,

I was a loose-dick eighteen-year-old boy who battled a constant pussy-drought as I searched desperately for a sliver of wetness in a sea of stingy teen girls.

"How do you know that *I* don't have anything?" she asked, her voice low but serious.

"Megan, I believed you when you said you'd become a recluse. I'm willing to bet you haven't had sex since your husband was killed. Your pussy is probably tighter than a virgin bride and wetter than a fucking dripping faucet right now."

She dropped her head, a tell-tale sign that I likely hit the nail on the head. I wasn't going to fuck her without a condom, but I'd be damned if it wasn't taking every ounce of my willpower to leave her alone. I stopped with a groan.

My dick was as hard as a steel support beam, but I managed to place Megan back on the floor and turn away from her quickly. I could feel her staring at my back, but I didn't look back. I couldn't. I needed to put some distance between us before I put action to my thoughts.

It had barely been forty-eight hours, and I had almost done the one thing my father had ordered me not to do. I swiped at the beads of sweat that had gathered at my hairline and forced myself to get as far away from Megan's tempting ass as I could get.

I didn't need to store up any firewood or chop it because I had only used my fireplace twice in three years. However, I was about to go and pick up an ax and start chopping down a lot of fucking trees. I needed to burn off this raging energy surging through me like supercharged electricity.

I had never reacted to a woman in that way. The way I was feeling right now, these fucking woods were about to catch hell.

CHAPTER ELEVEN

Aaron

The next day went by in a blur. My job, which was twenty-five miles away from my house, had thankfully kept me away from Megan, but it didn't stop me from wanting to fuck her. By nightfall, I became a crazed monster again, even crazier than the day prior.

We sat at my table, eating, the silence between us heavy enough to be another person in the room. Megan had avoided me most of the evening, but now while sitting in front of me with my eyes locked on her, she couldn't avoid my predatory gaze any longer.

I had barely touched my food, a sign of how amped up my need for her was. I watched her watching me and pretending like our sexual chemistry wasn't burning my damn house down to the ground.

My eyes wouldn't go anywhere but to her. My brain couldn't think past the desire swirling around in there like a tornado that needed to be set free. The only sounds in the room came from our clinking silverware and her phone spilling what I'm sure was an entertaining musical mix into the atmosphere.

She'd made meatloaf, which was good, but my desire overrode my taste buds and prevented me from enjoying the meal.

I tried. I promise, I fucking tried, but I couldn't take the anticipation anymore.

I released a loud growl that frightened Megan to the point of placing her hand over her heart. She stared at me like I'd lost my damn mind. I stood and stalked over her like a fucking madman. My forearm collided with our unfinished meals from me brushing it out of the way.

My sharp eyes remained locked on her as she watched the table's contents hit the floor, clinking and shattering. I reached into my back pocket and came out with a sleeve of condoms that I slapped down on top of the table where her plate once was.

Megan stared at me. Those big flirty eyes of hers were wide and her body frozen. I didn't know if she was frozen in fear or lust at this point. Hell, I didn't give a flying fuck anymore. She had masterfully seduced me whether she meant to or not.

"I can't fucking take it anymore, Megan. Can I fuck you or what?"

She stared at me, motionless and stunned like a deer in the headlights. One of her hands cupped her open mouth. The other remained over her heaving chest. She glanced around at the mess I made of our dinner before her gaze landed back on mine.

At this point, I was so fucking hot and bothered, my left eye was twitching. It usually only got this way when I was extremely pissed, ready to kick someone's ass, or right before I murdered someone.

In this case, it started twitching because I hadn't fucked a woman in four damn months and being around Megan had ignited an inferno within me. I was an asshole biker, but even I had standards. I didn't touch any of the women in my neck of the woods with a fucking ten-foot pole.

I heard the whispers of what they said about me behind my back. *"Aaron acts like he's too good for any of the women in Copper County. We ain't good enough for him."*

Fucking right! I'd rather beat my shit off than stick it in any of that nasty trash that hung around, throwing their pussy at anything with a swinging dick.

Megan was *different.* I noticed it the instant I saw her. She was one of those good girls who could be swayed to do bad shit if she met the right man. And the right one was *me.*

She hadn't answered my question, and despite how crazy she was causing me to act, I still had enough of my senses left to ask for permission first.

"Megan!"

My shout caused her to jump and bump the table. She was taking too damn long to answer me, but I couldn't force myself on her. I *wouldn't.* It was the one line I refused to cross although she had me acting like a ferocious animal because I wanted her so fucking bad. I was sure I hadn't misread that she wanted me yesterday when I pinned her on the countertop. *Had I?*

"Megan, I'm waiting for an answer."

She nodded and, "Yes," finally tumbled softly from her lips.

It was all I needed to know. I intended to take her on the table, but it wasn't going to be sturdy enough. If she was half as good as I suspected, I needed my bed because I didn't intend to stop fucking her until she or I or the both of us ended up passed the fuck out.

After slapping my hand on the package of condoms, I gripped Megan's wrist and yanked her from her seat. Before I realized what I was doing, I'd snatched her up, and my other hand was under her thigh, lifting her. I slung her clean across my shoulder and carried her caveman style up the back stairs with swift purpose.

Everything was in my fucking way. I bumped the small table in the hallway that led to my bedroom and the lamp that sat on top of it fell sideways and landed against the wall. It didn't fall to the floor, but it sat there leaning against the wall.

My shoulder brushed the large painting that hung on the hallway wall, and it slipped off one of the hooks and clung to the wall, barely hanging on to the last hook. All the while, Megan's warm, soft body rested over my shoulder, her heavy breaths mixed with my hasty steps as I marched us closer to my destination.

I tore through my bedroom door, making it collide into the wall with a loud thud before it swung back our way. I tapped it open with the toe of my boot to keep it out of my way and didn't bother to close it as I moved closer to my bed.

Megan hung draped over my shoulder like a human scarf. I liked that she didn't complain, or fight, or wiggle free. It was more of the confirmation I needed that she was on board with what was about to happen. That tempting round ass of hers that I'd been eyeballing since day one was right next to my mouth.

Unable to resist the temptation, I turned my head and clinched a good chunk of it between my teeth. The small yelp she released after I bit her on the ass made me grin before I slung her onto my bed. The condoms landed next to her, and I was unable to stop my eager hands from skimming over her chest.

"Do you need to piss?"

She shook her head. Those fucking seductive eyes were on me again and seeing her in my bed made sweat pool on my top lip.

I decided to step away and walked into my bathroom, figuring I better take a piss now before we got started. After washing my hands, I splashed cold water on my face. My skin was hot like I had caught lust fever.

I had never been like this before ravenous and cagey like a fucking feral animal. I needed to calm down. I'd likely already scared Megan half to death. The last thing I wanted was for her to change her shaky yes into a firm no.

A little less crazed, I walked back into my room. The creaking bed made the only noise when I sat next to Megan. She'd had her eyes on me the entire time. I sat so close to her that she had to place her hand on my thigh to stay upright.

And just like that, when her small warm hand gripped my thigh, my dick jumped, craving a part of the action. I was doing the best that I could with what little control I had left not to act like a sex-deprived crazy man.

"You want me to take off your clothes?" I asked, attempting to sound normal, but my breathy words sounded strained and forced.

At those words, Megan began the process of pulling off her top layers at a lingering pace like she was still unsure. I was not the least bit timid, shy, or reluctant. I threw my shirt over my head in one smooth, quick motion while kicking off my boots. I unzipped and dropped my pants before shoving them and my boxers down faster than you could hit a lick at a snake.

When I stood, bare-ass naked in front of her, Megan's gaze landed on my dick and remained there a *long* time. I didn't move. I wanted her to get a good look at what I was about to hit her with. She needed to know what she had said yes to.

When she finally started moving again, she revealed to me layer by layer the beautiful body she kept hidden under those sweats. My hands ached to caress her silky brown skin and those lush curves. Instead of skin and bones, she had a body a man could stroke, squeeze, and spank.

She kept her eyes on mine while reaching back to unclasp her bra. Was she moving that damn slowly on purpose? The smiling glint in her seductive eyes made me believe so. She hadn't said much in our exchange so far, but her body language was delivering a sermon that could incite the holy spirit.

After roving over my body, her gaze landed on my dick again. She swallowed as her posture tensed and her gaze remained on my dick while she slid her pants over her ankles.

I knew why she was tense. About ten inches of thick dick was why. Some women told me they didn't want to deal with *that thing*. They said they didn't want me to stretch them and ruin them for other men.

Frankly, I didn't know what the fuck they were afraid of. Everything I ever learned about pussy said it could take a good pounding and bounce back to normal afterwards.

Megan didn't need to worry her pretty little head because I would make sure I took good care of her.

"Don't worry. I'm not going to hurt you," I reassured her when reluctance seemed like it had crept into her head.

My words eased a little of her tension. I reached for her hand, and when she took mine, I tugged her up to stand so I could help her out of her last few stitches of clothes.

Her purple bra was unclasped but remained clinging to her chest. Those purple panties played up her bronzed skin tone, making me appreciate the beauty of it even more. Was purple her favorite color? It damn sure was mine when it was on her.

After pulling her in closer, I placed one of her hands on my side and the other on my hard dick. It pleased me to see I didn't have to give her blow-by-blow instructions. Delicate fingers stroked my dick from the base to the tip, as her gaze finally rose to meet mine again.

That's it, baby. Don't be afraid.

The more she loosened up, her hands grew firmer around my dick. The sensation of her soft caresses sliding over my hardness closed my eyes.

Without opening my eyes, I reached up and slid that bra down her arms. She let go of my dick long enough to let the bra fall from her arms and land at our feet.

Fuck if she wasn't perfect from her head to her purple toenails. Her perky round tits were full, and the hard dark-brown tips were begging for my mouth. I bent and took one of the tips into my mouth as my free hand massaged the other. She didn't let go of my dick, a sign that she was getting into this as much as me.

When my warm lips locked around her nipple, the action drew a low moan from her. The sound of her moaning for me thrilled me in a way that I hadn't expected. I brushed my tongue across one hard tip before I let my hand slide down the rest of her intoxicatingly smooth body.

She was a mixture of silk and cotton. My fingers looped into the waistband of her panties as my tongue snaked down her neck. Reluctantly, I drew my tongue away from her tasty skin when I bent to slide her panties down her sexy legs. This woman was pure seduction, everything you could ever need in one beautiful package.

My desperate gaze swept the expanse of her body from my downed view. My tongue slid across her lower lips when I noticed she didn't have any hair on her pussy. Her deep gasp at my action motivated me further, and I licked her there again while keeping my eyes locked on hers.

When I stood, I lifted her up in one swift motion. Her legs wrapped around my waist and her hot pussy sat above my stiff dick which was at full salute at this point. I climbed into my bed with her attached to me. My bed groaned under our weight, and the mattress springs punched me in the knees as I maneuvered us closer to the headboard.

Megan had no idea that she was the first woman I ever had in my bed, and I damn sure wasn't about to tell her. I didn't want anyone to know where I lived, and most of the women I took an interest in were usually one-night stands that I met and fucked in cheap motels as far away from Copper County as I could get.

I sat Megan in front of my wooden headboard, reluctantly breaking our connection.

"Turn around, get on your knees, and hold onto the headboard," I instructed.

***

Megan

Fear shot through me like fireworks, but at the same time, Aaron turned me on enough to leave me dripping wet. He was right in his assessment. The more he scared me, the more it heightened my arousal. This was a side of me I never explored. I was a bit of a thrill seeker, enjoying rides and stunts that got my heart pumping, but the type of buzz Aaron was giving me was new.

I did as he had instructed, turning my anxious body until my shaky hands gripped the headboard. At first, my hands shook because I was nervous, now they shook because I was aroused. God, his dick was so *big*.

From behind, a shark circled, and my body was ripe enough for him to sink his teeth into, or better yet, that big-ass dick of his. I feared the amount of pain surely coming my way. The craziest thing about this situation is although I knew it would hurt, I remained ready to endure whatever came next. Was that fucking twisted or what?

The mattress springs cried under his weight as he moved closer to me. His lips grazed over my shoulder, making me suck in a deep breath. I glanced back to figure out his intentions when he eased back.

He laid down on his back behind me and slid his face under the lower half of my body. His warm breath blew against my pussy and sent a chill up my spine, but he didn't stop his movement. His shoulders connected with my inner thighs, and he continued to inch higher until his face was at my chest.

The next thing I knew, his hot tongue slid over my hard nipples. He gripped my hips, and before I could think, he bench pressed me.

He lifted me so quickly; I gasped and tightened my grip on the headboard as he aligned my pussy with his mouth. His hot breath was back at my aching cove, and I was moaning before he even caressed me.

When his lips glided over my now dripping, wet pussy, and his strong tongue caressed my clit, I gasped before releasing a strangled cry.

"Oh my God!"

I'd never had my pussy eaten in this position, but it was proving to be highly effective. The scruffiness of his beard, the warm softness of his lips, and the firm slippery strokes of his tongue sparked a unique brand of pleasure that he should consider patenting. I relished every stroke of his magnificent tongue when he licked the inner and outer edges of my lips and proceeded to brush it over my clit before sliding it inside me.

My harsh breathing was only a step down from hyperventilating. My moaning mixed with the smacking of his lips and the slurps of his hungry mouth. Aaron was eating me like I was the first meal he'd had in months.

"Your pussy tastes so fucking good," he commented before he went right back to feasting on me. Hearing his admission only made me burn hotter and my juices flow faster.

I was literally melting on his tongue and falling deeper into the throes of the most delightful haze of pleasure I had ever experienced. My bent knees rested over Aaron's shoulders, but he supported most of my weight by controlling the grip he had on my thighs. It had only been minutes, and I was already about to explode all over his face. My body had a mind of its own, dancing against his face as I thrust my pussy at his mouth.

My moans were a mixture of heaving breaths and strangled cries. "Shit. Oh God!" I gripped the varnished dark wood of his headboard so tight that it was a wonder I hadn't gotten a splinter. When my body began to tremble, I slammed my eyes shut and let his impressive tongue flick me over the edge.

The orgasm wrecked me, causing me to fall into a boneless heap over the headboard as I continued to shiver and thrust.

Aaron didn't give me time to recover. I continued to shake from the effects of my orgasm while he eased me down. He laid me out in front of him, on my back, as I continued to struggle to get air into my lungs.

He ripped off a condom from the package and rolled it over his dick so fast you would have thought he was being timed. He kneeled before me, gripping my hips and tugging me so that my inner thighs met the outside of his.

I noticed he hadn't bent over me, wanting to see his dick going into me. Fuck, if I didn't want to see it too. He sat the tip at my soaking, wet slit and gave me a quick glance before he shoved past my quivering wet folds.

The action made me drop into the mattress as my eyes slammed shut. His thrust was forceful, delivering a sweet pain I didn't mind.

He moved at a lingering pace to open me. The pressure and the pleasure it sparked and the lusty ache he delivered made me want all of him inside.

My head shot up to get a look when he drew all the way back out. The way his eyes made love to my body, the way his muscles bulged and rippled under his skin, the way his taut warm skin made my fingertips tingle while sliding over it. All of this need, the intense desire, it enticed me, swayed me into submission, letting me know that I was starving for this when I didn't even know I was hungry for it.

He gave me just enough time to miss the sweet, hard pressure before he shoved his dick back in. This time, most of it slid into my wet, tight pussy. I barely knew this man, but I was so deep under Aaron's spell that I didn't care how long it took or how hard he fucked me. I intended to lay there and take it all.

He repeated the thrust, moving faster now and sliding in and all the way out, over and over, giving me a gift set on repeat. Our breathing mingled, rushing out heavy and hard. The mattress screamed under our dancing weight, making a chorus of sound that echoed throughout the room.

Aaron growled between gritted teeth and heaving breaths, his words broken but understandable.

"Your fucking sweet pussy is better than I imagined."

He slammed into me this time, burying every inch inside of me, which was something I didn't think possible. "Shit. Your pussy is so fucking good," he whispered with clenched eyes as his nails dug deeper into my hips with every hard thrust.

I was stunned by the shock of his powerful thrust and the unbelievable fact that he'd gotten all that dick inside me without ruining something. And I'd be damned if his dick didn't create the most addicting high I ever experienced.

He had a reach that stroked areas I didn't know could be stroked. My cries were ripped from my throat by a force I couldn't see. I gripped the sheets one second and his back the next. I could tell by the bruising grip of my fingers that I was leaving marks on him. He made me lose my damn mind, the first time in my life that I didn't mind relinquishing my sanity.

Thrusting into me with hard, sure strokes, Aaron had reached clean to the back of my pussy. The ache of my second orgasm made me scream, "Aaron, you're fucking me so good! Please don't stop!" I begged for it, shouting my desperate pleas into the sexually charged air we created.

The orgasm hit like a series of detonated explosives that took my mind and body on an adventure. Aaron rocked me with enough force that I swore I had fallen clean through to the other side of life. He made me see rainbows and unicorns and experience the kind of ecstasy that had the power to possess one's soul.

He cheered me on. "That's right, baby, cum all over this dick," he growled the demand between desperate breaths. I continued to overdose on the sparks of euphoria flooding my system while my pussy clenched and pulsed around his dick.

"Fuck! So, fucking good…so fucking…"

Aaron's loud roar sounded as his dick thundered inside me. His body jerked as his dick spewed his hot cum into the condom, pulsing inside me with enough pressure to bring on another orgasm. I couldn't say anything. My mouth was stuck wide open as I let the sensations take me.

After a few minutes of us lying there in the aftermath of the most explosive sex I ever experienced, Aaron finally pulled out of me. I shook at his exit.

I immediately missed him being inside me and didn't hesitate to watch him get up and walk into the bathroom.

Splayed out over his bed, I was too weak to move my satisfied body. That wasn't at all what I'd expected. After I managed to lift and place my shaky fingers over my warm face, all I could think was, *Fuck, I think I'm hooked.*

***

Aaron

After I threw the condom in the toilet and flushed it, I washed my dick off with a wet, soapy towel. I took a few deep breaths before I glanced at my reflection in the mirror. I washed my hands before slapping cold water on my hot face that had turned three shades of red.

"What the fuck have you done, Aaron? You know you're in trouble, right?"

I shook my head at my reflection, knowing I had just opened a box that would be a motherfucker to close. In a way, I understood why my father didn't want me fucking Megan. One hit was all it had taken, and I was a fucking addict with the first stroke.

I'd had the most explosive sex of my life with the one woman I was forbidden to touch. It had been drilled into my head my entire life that I was to never fuck a black woman. I assumed it was because my family was a bunch of racist assholes, but now I was beginning to think that there were ulterior motives behind their rules.

My father acted his part of the racist asshole well. He'd fooled me most of my life, but he forgot I had witnessed the way he interacted with people in certain situations where he could have been the monster he portrayed. And a bigoted asshole was not what I saw. I always believed he was hiding something from me, from all of us. Why choose to hide behind a veil of hate that I don't believe was genuine?

It was also drilled into my head never to do drugs because of the damage they could do to your mind and body. Yet, I feared I'd introduced myself to one of the most addictive drugs that existed. There wasn't a damn thing I could do about it now because all I wanted at this moment was to return to my bedroom and fuck Megan again and again and a fucking 'gain.

When I gathered my wits enough to walk back into the room, I found her putting her clothes back on. I stood over her, shaking my head as the cool air from the vent above rained over my hot body. My dick was becoming harder from the sight of her.

"You may as well take that shit back off," I told her. "We are not done."

Megan didn't even protest or ask any questions. She knew our shit together was good because she proceeded to take her clothes right back off.

This time when I made her face the headboard, I fucked her from behind, and I'll be damned if this time didn't wreck my fucking mind as good as the first time.

Like the crazed addict I was, I alternated between eating Megan's pussy and fucking her. I squeezed three more rounds out of her before she said, "I think my pussy is too sore to go again."

CHAPTER TWELVE

Aaron

My eight-hour shift at work had flown by in a blur. I received funny looks from my men when I volunteered to do the tedious shit they hated doing like filing and making rounds by foot.

There was a massive influx of fucking energy coursing through me, and I was so light on my feet I had to force myself to relax before the men figured out what kind of fucking drug I was on—Megan.

She had me acting out of character, giddy, and smiling for no fucking reason. I rarely smiled, so the men stared at me with concern, likely thinking I had lost my natural mind.

I could hardly wait to get off work so I could get another hit. I prayed Megan's soreness had dwindled because I needed more. The idea of more sex with her made me anxious as fuck.

When I finally made it home that evening, my father was sitting in my living room with a plate of Megan's food in his hands. I wanted to kick his ass out of my house so I could have what I was craving all day. Instead, I poured my energy into keeping my cool when my drug of choice stepped into the living room. She handed my father a glass of lemonade and turned to me.

"Are you ready to eat?"

Fuck yes. I'm ready to eat. You.

I nodded without looking up at her. She walked away without another word. My father eyeballed me like he knew something was up.

"How are things going with her? I see she's cleaned this place from top to bottom. She ain't a lazy bitch. I can tell you that much," he commented before he fell quiet and continued eating.

I remained silent, watching him.

"I came to talk to you about your punk-ass cousins. They didn't have your money. I was tempted to kick their asses myself, but I found out they used the money to pay for a medical procedure for their mother. It's why they've been coming up short recently. I confirmed it, and apparently, their mother has a blood disorder. Jake used the money, knowing he would get into trouble to cover her medical expenses. Long story short, he doesn't have the rest of your money. The only thing I can suggest is you hang on to Macon for another week, which will take her nearly to the end of her month. She could be yours until your cousins are in the clear or can give you the balance of what you think they owe you."

You have no fucking idea. I've already been paid in full.

My father raised an eyebrow like he heard my inner thoughts. I didn't need the money my cousins owed me, but I'd been trying for years to get them to be more responsible in the way they handled business.

I shifted in my seat when Megan walked in with my plate. My gaze remained on the plate she handed me, but when my hand slid over hers, the plate wobbled and nearly toppled to the floor. I shot a quick glance at my father to see if he noticed my fumble, but Shark was too busy eating to notice me fail to hide my weakness over my living addiction. I glanced up at Megan who held her shit together like nothing had happened between us.

"Thank you."

"You're welcome," she said in her normal low tone before handing me the glass of lemonade. The only time she had broken away from that soft church-lady tone of hers was when I was fucking her.

My father's gaze was on Megan's ass as she walked away, and I didn't like that shit one bit. My forehead creased. I knew I had no damn reason to be possessive, but I was nevertheless.

Why? Why the fuck would I be possessive about any woman? What the fuck was happening?

My father eyed me once more, his gaze boring into me.

"What do you think? Keep Mellissa for another week until your cousins get you your money? She's probably safer out here with you anyway. It was only a matter of time before I'd have to beat the hell out of one of the club members for trying to fuck her. I mean, I've got my issues with black people, but that one… She'll make you forget the rules."

What rules?

My ears perked up. My father's admission made me curious to know more about those two weeks Megan had spent at the club. He pointed his crooked thumb toward my kitchen.

"The first few days, I thought I would have to tell her to get the hell on and find another way to pay off her sister's debt. Her presence had unsettled the delicate balance we fight to maintain. But after she picked up that damn gun and proved herself, the entire vibe changed. Believe it or not, a few of the guys have been asking for her, telling me they miss her cooking and shit."

I forked a hardy helping of Megan's shrimp pasta mix into my mouth. There was one thing I knew for sure. If a club member had fucked Megan, they'd be at my door right now attempting to kidnap her ass. And, what was up with my father calling her every name but *Megan*? The shit was weird but pointing it out would only agitate him.

I nodded at his suggestion that Megan stay with me. "Yeah, that will be fine. She can stay."

Now, will you go the hell away from here so I can fuck her?

***

Megan

I finished my meal but remained sitting at the kitchen table, waiting for Shark to leave. Was Aaron and I going to do it again? I had never had sex that many times in one night before and I damn sure had never cum that many times in one night. I didn't even know it was possible.

Was it bad of me to want him to *fuck*—as Aaron would say—me again? I loved my dearly departed husband, God rest his soul, but he was always delicate during sex. He acted like he would break me or something.

Aaron was rough and hard and intoxicating. He drove me to my limits with the way he pounded into me so hard and good. It was like he demanded my enjoyment of his sex.

His commanding eyes, the strength of his attitude, even his scent turned me on. He was raw and rugged and handsome and sexy all at the same time. Aaron didn't bother wearing cologne although he had several bottles in his bathroom. Remnants of the soap, shampoo, and the deodorant he used along with his natural, intoxicating male scent were more than enough to lure my senses in and draw me to him with ease.

When Aaron stepped into the kitchen, his gaze locked with mine. He stepped up to me and slapped a piece of paper on the table just as he had done with the condoms the day before. After he placed his dishes in the sink, he walked back over to the table and stood over me.

My eyes refused to drop away from him. His button-up white shirt and black slacks were a part of his work uniform but seeing him in something other than jeans gave him a refreshing appeal.

His hair was gelled back and away from his face and tied back with a rubber band. With his hair combed back, the strong features of his handsome face were more visible, making him even more desirable.

When my gaze dropped from his face to the document on the table, my mouth fell open. It was his medical clearance form, confirming that he was free of all STD's.

I glanced up, speechless. How the hell had he gotten this report in one day?

"Small town. I know the doctor and lab tech," he answered like he was reading my mind. He had already started undoing the buttons on his shirt.

After last night, I could understand why he would want to fuck me with no barriers between us. Shit, truth be told, I was probably as curious as him. Obviously, he was trusting that I had a clean bill of health as well. What did he see in me to trust me that much?

"So, can I fuck you with no condom?" he asked. He was direct and self-doubt was a concept lost on him.

His chiseled chest peeked out from the two halves of his open shirt. I threw my hands up, torn between shock and fuck-yes-ness. Instead, I remained calm.

"I suppose so," I told him, struggling not to let my lust-filled gaze trail down his body and linger at his dick that had tented in his pants. It wasn't the answer I wanted to give, but I couldn't let him know that thinking about him had my pussy throbbing all day.

"That's a good enough answer for me," he stated.

He didn't give me time to say another word. He snatched me from my seat, hiked me up onto the counter, and didn't waste a moment dragging my sweats over my dangling legs. The kicker wasn't even that he wanted me so badly. It was that I wanted him just as much, if not *more*.

I helped him by heaving my shirt over my head and dropping it on the floor as he slid my panties down my legs. My ass kissed the cold, smooth surface of the counter, but my body was so warm, it would likely leave a dewy layer of frost where I sat.

Aaron tore off his shirt, popping a few of the buttons off the arms as he slung it off his shoulders before tugging it over his wrists. He didn't even bother taking his pants all the way off. He yanked them and his boxers down to his thighs, far enough for his dick to jump up and point right where it wanted to be—right inside my slick, hot, and throbbing pussy.

Two things happened quickly. Aaron slid my ass to the edge of the counter and thrust into me in one long and smooth stroke that took my breath away. My fingers dug into his tight muscular biceps as my head landed on the edge of his shoulder. It was a damn shame that I was so weak with need and so full of burning lust that I could barely hold my own head up.

Aaron didn't care if I was ready or not. He didn't hold back as he began to pound into me. I gasped, nearly choking on the large amount of oxygen that flooded my lungs. Before I could exhale, the hypnotic sensations his dick induced took over my body.

I clenched my already shut eyes tighter as they rolled to the back of my head. I lifted my head, but it fell back quickly as my mouth dropped open, allowing my ragged breaths to fill the kitchen.

My fingernails on one hand dug deeper into Aaron's taut bicep and the other dug into the side of his rippling abdominal muscles as I assisted in pulling him further between my splayed legs.

Deep cries of pleasure accompanied every sinful stroke that touched me deep inside with no barrier between us. This encounter was a magical mixture that had no business existing. I was gone after the first stroke, but the longer he drove that strong, pulsing and sensational dick into me, the further I traveled away from rationale and reason.

I lost control of my moans and vocal cries. If Shark came back for any reason and caught us, I didn't think Aaron would stop. Even worse, I wouldn't want him to stop.

Shark would see us fucking in Aaron's kitchen and hear me saying, "Oh my God, Aaron, that feels so good. Keep fucking me like that."

My pleas were cut short as a violent quiver started at my stomach and rolled up and over my chest, making my entire body convulse.

"Fuck. Fuck. Fuck. Megan. Fuck! It's better than I could have imagined. Shhhiiit!"

He dragged out the word, *shit*, like it had five syllables instead of one. His grunts and *fucks* never stopped as he pounded into me with hungry thrusts that struck the back of me with each dip his dick took inside me. The slapping sound of his hips against my inner thighs livened up the otherwise quiet kitchen.

Aaron didn't have to tell me to open myself for him. I spread my legs as wide as I could get them, allowing him the space he needed to fuck me as hard and as fast as he desired. At this point, I was so strung out that I forgot that anything but us existed.

He lifted me by placing both his hands under my ass, easily holding my weight so that he stayed buried deep inside as he rotated his hips with lingering deep thrusts that drove me crazier than I already was. He moved me so that I rode his dick while he remained impaled, massaging everything inside me.

"I don't want out of this pussy. It's so fucking good!" he confessed. His loud and boisterous shouts vibrated through me even as I caught fire for him and danced atop his deeply planted iron-hard dick. I'd never experienced anything like this before; sex so good it literally made me lose my sanity.

We may as well have been animals in the wild because we fucked without inhibitions—no remorse or regret. Aaron's hair had fallen loose from the band he'd tied around it, and it bobbed in time with his thrusting hips and teased the side of my face and neck.

He stroked everything, sparking intense vibrations and I became a woman possessed. With Aaron, I indulged in my greatest impulses, and I wasn't ashamed of my lustful and wanton actions. I was free, unhinged from what kept me tied to any semblance of decency.

"Aaron, I'm about to cum all over your dick. Oh, God, help me!"

I choked on the massive amount of pleasure he forced into my body, unable to suck in a full breath. I was on the verge of a heart attack or another condition that would cause me to go into shock.

My heart was about to stop. I knew it was. The buildup of the orgasm was so intense that I was almost afraid to let go, but I didn't have a choice. It swept through me, taking me by force.

Words I didn't understand flew out of my mouth. Somehow, I endured the blast, as total earth-shattering bliss consumed me and took me to another world.

"Oh! Fuck! Your pussy is pounding so hard baby. I can't...I can't..."

I vaguely caught Aaron's roaring words as they filled the interior of his kitchen. He was taken by one of those blissful explosions that had taken me. He pounded into me so fast and hard it sounded like a drummer finding the right rhythm for his bass drum.

Just as he gifted me the night before and just as my orgasm started to subside, his dick pulsed so wantonly inside me that it enticed another orgasm that seized my body and left me a jerking mass of flesh, unconscious of how I acted or sounded.

We allowed ourselves only a few minutes and although exhausted from our previous night's activities, we managed two more pleasure-filled rounds in Aaron's bed before he allowed me to fall asleep.

When I rose to get up to go to my room, Aaron pulled me right back down and snuggled me against his chest before he passed out. Like everything else between us, this was unexpected.

Weren't we just *fucking*? As a matter of fact, I preferred *just fucking* with no care and concern to worry about. When it was time for me to go, the last thing I wanted was to have formed an attachment to him. I was sure I was already addicted to the man's dick.

Aaron delivered the best sex I ever experienced, but something that good wasn't meant to be shared long-term. Despite my reluctance at being folded into his strong arms, I relaxed into the warm confines of his solid chest. His arms tightened around me as I nuzzled closer, and my eyes drifted closed.

CHAPTER THIRTEEN

Aaron

This type of shit wasn't supposed to be happening. I was taking a crash course in the only class that had ever held my interest: Megan 101. Getting her to speak about herself was as tough as pulling teeth with my fingers. However, I did learn that she enjoyed cooking and trying new recipes due to her not being allowed to do so in foster care.

It sounded like a simple statement but the emotion she failed to hide said the system had been a lot harder on her than she was willing to say.

Currently in the kitchen with her, I watched her cook. Occasionally, I helped her but the tags remained on some of my pots and pans, revealing how often I prepared my own food. I handed her the pan she asked for and walked to the refrigerator to get the butter.

"So, what made you want to cook? You don't have any kids or family and there were so many other activities you could have picked?"

I was fishing. She dropped her head for a second and the haunting look that crossed her face disappeared as quickly as it had surfaced. She was good at hiding her emotions.

"I liked pretending that I was cooking for the kind of family I always wanted and knew I would never have. People laughed and talked and forgot about their problems around good food. I saw it all the time, but I never really ever got a chance to experience it. So..." She shrugged.

"You pretended, even if it was just you," I finished.

She nodded and returned to mixing what I believed was cornbread into a big bowl.

An hour later and stuffed, I sat with her on the couch, still asking periodic questions that she continued to deflect. When I started massaging her foot, her head fell back, and her eyes closed.

The sight of her enjoyment put another rare smile on my face. I believed I'd smile more in the last few days than I had my entire life. If she allowed me to keep fucking her the way I wanted, I was willing to give her any kind of massage she desired.

***

Two days later.

Although neither Megan nor I were big talkers, it didn't take away from our connection. We got each other whether we exchanged words or not. However, there were times when Megan would go quiet on me, even quieter than usual.

She would lay her head against my shoulder or chest and allow her fingers to trace the lines and curves of my tattoos. When her fingers weren't on me, she made me tingle with her tongue. I wasn't sure yet if it was her way to get me to stop questioning her or if it was all attraction.

There weren't many areas left on me that she hadn't explored. It almost seemed like she was studying me, memorizing every line and angle of my body.

Like now, her fingers slunk over the lines of the metal skull on my back. Soon after, her tongue glazed over the dull red scales of the diamondback slithering over my shoulder. The head of the snake stopped at my right pec, and so did her tongue.

I was bitten by a diamondback rattler as part of a torture session after I was captured by one of my MC's adversaries. The snake had bitten me twice, and the venom should have killed me after I was beaten, thrown into a shallow hole, and left for dead. It was a deadly mistake on the group's part that they hadn't made sure I was dead.

Megan's movement drew my attention away from images of torture and revenge. I never had anyone, especially not a woman, pay this much attention to me. This experience was foreign, uncomfortable, yet sensual in a way. It's why I didn't make her stop when she concentrated on me like this. It turned me on, but I wasn't necessarily roaring to plant one of my heads between her legs.

"What are you doing?" I asked after her fingers trailed over the black printed Scripture covering my left side and along my abs. It was from I John, the first chapter and the ninth verse, which read, 'He frees us from the slavery of sin and sets us free to experience new life.' Lord knew I, more than anyone, needed to be set free of sin. I also knew and accepted that I couldn't do it on my own.

"Remembering," she finally answered my question. She continued the meticulous movement of her delicate fingers until her index finger circled the bloody exit wound tattoo on my lower left side.

The tattoo covered an actual exit wound from the first gunshot that ever pierced my body. I'd taken the shot to my lower back, saving my cousin Ansel. The bullet had pinged off one of my bones and exited through my side. There was a small entrance wound tattooed on my lower back where the bullet had entered.

Megan's gaze rolled over and rested on the blood-stained handcuff tattooed around my left wrist. Her eyebrows knitted tighter when her gaze rose and landed on the name, 'Ryan,' tattooed in black cursive letters atop a bricked headstone on my forearm.

I was compelled to share the story of my younger brother with Megan, but I stopped myself. We should be fucking each other, not sharing personal stories. On second thought, we shouldn't be fucking each other either, but I couldn't help myself on that front.

Did I almost just tell her about my brother? Ryan had been shot in the head during a shootout we had with a rival MC. He was a few weeks shy of his thirteenth birthday at the time, and I was fifteen. Although Ryan didn't have a gun, most of our MC had guns in their hands returning fire. Therefore, we couldn't go to any law enforcement agency to seek legal justice for him.

Ryan's death weighed heavily on me. I was the closest to him when he died. He was standing right next to me. I never shared it with the rest of my family, but I truly believed Ryan had died protecting me that day. He was ducking behind a stack of old tires right next to me when one of our enemies snuck up on us.

Things happened so fast I had no proof other than what I think may have happened. I believe Ryan stood and took that bullet to protect me. I believe he stared death in the face to keep his big brother from getting shot.

Ryan meant everything to me. He was a good kid who hadn't inherited the madness that roared inside of me, and I never forced him to embrace this life. For reasons I have yet to understand, he looked up to me like I was the best thing in his life. He told me I was the bravest and smartest person he knew and that he was glad he had a big brother like me. It should have been *me* protecting Ryan that evening and not the other way around.

It took my father and me two years to track down the man who'd killed Ryan. I was so relentless in my pursuit of my brother's killer that I stopped at nothing to hunt him down. I even dropped out of school for a while. My actions during that time had earned me the nickname Grave Digger.

By seventeen, I had killed more men than some of our seasoned members. My actions prompted the chairmen at the time to vote and name me one of the club's enforcers. I killed five of the rival MC's men before I found the one who shot Ryan. Every time I killed one of them, I would reopen the grave and add each additional dead member to the pile of bodies stacking up.

Megan's tongue sliced across my nipple and brought me out of my haunting memories. Her action made me suck in a harsh breath.

"It seems like you're studying me," I whispered.

She glanced up from scrutinizing the spent bullet shell casings that billowed smoke on the back of my left hand and flashed me a shy smile.

"I am."

My curiosity was piqued. "Why the heck would you want to study me?"

"Because I want to remember you," she said casually with her gaze locked with mine. "Everything about you."

The fuck?

Why the hell would she want to remember everything about a fucker like me? I wasn't the guy who inspired women to remember me. The most they were going to get was a good fuck followed by my asshole attitude telling them to get lost.

Megan was more like me than I think she knew. She was not the sentimental type. It was one of the things I liked about her. She didn't drag in the emotional baggage that women liked to bring into a sexual situation.

That being said, as unintentional as Megan may have been with her statements about wanting to remember everything about me, it had my fucking heart doing flip flops and banging all around in my damn chest.

As much as we avoided the emotional side of this affair, the shit still crept in from time to time anyway. Not even the rules and laws of Copper County or years of the dark history of hatred and cruelty my motorcycle club stood for was enough to stop Megan and me from wanting each other. I don't know if she harbored the same kind of want for me that I had for her, but I believe I was beginning to want every part of her—mind, body, and soul.

For God's sake, I was reading her books and shit. Not that I didn't study the hell out of shit that could give me any kind of advantage over an enemy. However, me reading a book for the hell of it wasn't a natural occurrence.

It took me less than two work days to finish one of her paranormal books. Surprisingly, I had enjoyed her spin on werewolves and had since downloaded two more of those addictive books of hers. Seeing the smile I'd put on her beautiful face after I'd informed her that I'd finished the first book, had pleased me.

CHAPTER FOURTEEN

Aaron

After we injected each other with the most addictive drug on the planet: our sex, Megan talked to me until I fell asleep. Time was the magic pill she needed to get her sexy lips moving around words versus my dick.

Sports, book ideas, music, what I did at work—we'd talk about everything. She still wasn't spilling many details about herself, but I believed time would inspire her to share more. Our sex could be bottled and sold as sleeping pills, so our conversations never lasted long after we exhausted ourselves on each other.

I appreciated her efforts to converse with me when I got the distinct impression that she would have been just fine without words. Her soothing, low tone relaxed me, but there was something else in her voice that sparked with hints of care and understanding.

Right now, I could hear the sleepiness in her dragging tone. Before she allowed herself to be lured into the dream world, she sank her fingers into my beard and gently massaged before she fell asleep cupping my chin.

A number of things that were a no-way-in-hell to other women, Megan was allowed, as she was the only one who could touch my beard.

I glanced down at her, fast-asleep and using my chest for her pillow. She grew tired of me taking her phone for her musical playlist, so she cloned it and downloaded it to my phone. She also suggested I start using the trendy apps to download music, but I didn't have time, nor was I that interested figuring it all out.

While at work today, I found myself texting her silly text messages and what were once rare smiles, turned into beaming grins each time I saw her replies. Who the fuck was this new Aaron and where had the real Aaron gone?

Texting, being silly, and enjoying the company of a woman was out of my character. Surely, I had lost my mind, and the craziest thing about the situation was I didn't give a flying fuck. For once in my life, I enjoyed something other than motorcycles, a good fight, and staring down the sight of a weapon aimed at an unlucky target.

Among the bits of information about herself that I was learning, I discovered that Megan enjoyed running. It was a rare piece of information I learned about her when she'd asked if it was safe to run in the sea of thick trees that surrounded my house. I told her no. I didn't want to risk anything happening to her.

I lowered my head, seeking out her warmth, but my lips ended up against her forehead in a delicate kiss. She released a contended sigh at my soft touch, before burrowing deeper into my chest. What the fuck was I doing?

***

Aaron

After work, I showed up at my house with a new treadmill for Megan. This was the first time I'd ever gotten anything for a woman in my personal life. The sound of Megan's laughter, the tight hugs and kisses of gratitude she bestowed on me did funny things to my heart.

This tugging at my heartstrings had to stop, I convinced myself. When Megan finally turned me loose, I distanced myself from her with another tree-chopping episode.

When I returned and Megan showed me how grateful she was for my gesture in other more sexual ways, I forgot all about stepping back. I allowed myself to fall further into the danger of the addiction I kept feeding.

We were playing a dangerous game of crossing a line that shouldn't be touched. We were acting like a couple. Is that what the fuck we were now, a couple?

***

Aaron

Today consisted of work and fucking Megan. First we did it in the living room and then on the stairs before we ended up in my bed. During our break she studied me the way she always did. She cooked for me and served me dinner before letting me fuck her on the kitchen table.

***

Megan

I ran on my new treadmill, cooked for Aaron, and made sure my pussy was shaved clean the way he told me he liked it. God, why was I encouraging him and not stopping this shit from going any deeper than it already was? We were catching feelings. I knew it and he knew it, but neither of us dared speak about it.

To be honest, I was enjoying these days I had with Aaron so much, I was beginning to regret that my remaining days with his MC were dwindling down. Never in my wildest dreams would I have believed my craziest idea ever would've turned into one of my most exciting. My time with Aaron had been the most enjoyable in a very long time.

Currently, we were on his couch, my head rested against his shoulders and my legs were thrown over his. He was massaging one of my feet, and I was loving every second of it.

"So, your full name is August Aaron Knox V, but you prefer using your middle name, Aaron," I said. It was a statement, me repeating what he'd just shared.

He nodded and a rare shyness flashed on his face. "I've never told anyone else. I believe my club brothers all believe Aaron is my name, unaware that I even have a middle name."

"So, this is privileged information?" I asked him, fighting those little flutters he incited every time he was sentimental with me. I wasn't sure if he even realized how intimate he was being with me.

I pointed at the tattoo that kept calling my attention.

"Will you tell me about this?"

His gaze lifted and met mine. His facial expression was unreadable, but the strength of something I believed was sorrow flashed in his gaze before he nodded.

He told me about his younger brother, Ryan, and it tore my heart apart because I empathized with the pain pouring from the depths of his gaze. He tried, but he couldn't hide how deeply he loved his little brother. The pain of his loss leaked between the syllables of his words. His words died after he informed me that they couldn't advocate justice for Ryan through legal means. I knew what that meant and didn't press him for an explanation. After he said about as much as he would say about Ryan, he changed the subject to his grandfather.

Aaron's grandfather was who started the club after he returned from WWII back in 1946. His grandfather claimed that he'd seen too much action in the war to return to the quiet life of a butcher, so he started the August Knights Motorcycle Club. Most of the Knox men joined the military, either for the training or to pay homage to their MC's founder.

I was enjoying him and his life too much. At some point I needed to start distancing myself. At first, he was reluctant to share his personal life. Now that it crossed my mind, it concerned me how much of his life he was sharing.

There was no way I was sharing any of my personal information with Aaron other than what he already knew. I didn't need or want him tracking me down when the time came for me to leave.

If he somehow found me after my thirty days of working for his MC was completed, there was no guarantee that I wouldn't follow him anywhere he wanted me to go. So, I would let caution be my guide and avoid the personal stuff.

***

Aaron

I surprised Megan and drove home for my lunch break. I snuck into my garage and caught her running her little heart out on that treadmill. Was she working out to stay fit or to stay strong and in shape for another reason?

Sometimes it seemed she was training for a secret mission that only she knew about. I even caught her practicing punches and kicks, doing push-ups, sit-ups, and all sorts of strengthening and muscle-building exercises.

Either way, her efforts were paying off because her body was pure perfection. Like now, I licked my lips at the sight of sweat glistening on her brown skin.

Unable to help my fucking self, I dragged her off the treadmill, mid-stride. With her music plugged in, I fucked her against my garage wall. I refused to allow her to take out her music, which made the episode so much more intense.

It was the best and only sweaty-exercise sex I ever experienced.

***

Aaron

Megan got her period today; a modified version of it at least. Since she had that birth control device implanted in her arm, she voluntarily shared that her period never lingered for more than a day or two. She called it spotting or something. I didn't understand it and had no intention of asking for the details.

Megan didn't let whatever was happening to her body stop her from giving me the best head of my life, though. I was getting so much pussy lately that I forgot about the other ways you could enjoy sex. Long story short, today I found out that Megan's mouth was as big an addiction as her sweet pussy.

CHAPTER FIFTEEN

Megan

I padded to the door wearing only one of Aaron's T-shirts and a pair of purple panties. There was no need for my sweats anymore. Aaron was only going to rip them off as soon as he entered his house.

A suffocating gasp hissed from my throat after I swung the door open and my gaze swept over three, big-ass men who looked like life had given them hell, standing on the porch. They didn't utter a word, but their slow-scanning gapes raked over my body and left me feeling like I needed to wash myself in a pool of bleach.

Beards, dirty jeans, black boots, and leather vests covered black turtleneck T-shirts and made the three look like evil twins. The one with the longest beard had enough nerve to lick his lips at me suggestively. It was funny how these people claimed to hate black people, but when they saw an African American woman who piqued their interest, they lost their fucking minds.

The one with the shortest beard had a cold sore on his lip that was ready to pop. His beard was patchy like he'd been bitten by a wild stray and caught the mange or something. My gaze traveled back to the cold sore, despite how much their dangerous presence alarmed me.

Medium beard was the first to speak. "Who the fuck are you and where the fuck is Aaron?"

My excessive staring and hard swallowing prevented me from answering the question right away. Smudges of dirt and grime clung to their faces and necks. Where the hell had these men come from, the inside of someone's chimney? There was so much dirt under one's nails it appeared he'd painted the tips black.

The stench of body odor sailed up my nostrils, and I was forced to choke down the gag that climbed up my throat. The funk and the cold sore made it difficult for me to concentrate. I attempted to formulate an escape plan in my head, but nothing that made sense would come together.

I decided to shoot from the hip until my brain decided to piece itself back together and come up with something that might save me from the vile shit about to go down.

"I'm the maid, and Aaron's personal property," I expressed, with the straightest face I could muster. "He'll be home from work in a little bit."

With a hand gesture, I ushered them in because I didn't know what else to do. There was no use telling them they couldn't come in. Their stern, aggressive vibe revealed that they were there to start shit, no matter what I said or did.

Aaron's house was way off the beaten path; so far off, that you probably wouldn't find it even if you were lost. I remember Aaron mentioning that his house was not even under his name, so if anyone came looking for him who wasn't from his MC, they were looking for trouble or bringing it.

A breeze that I hadn't noticed during my entire stay in Copper County blew against my bare legs and reminded me that I was only in Aaron's T-shirt, panties, and no bra. The T-shirt reached midways down my thighs, which thankfully, covered enough of me that it could have been a mini dress. Nevertheless, I did my best to swallow my nervousness.

I glanced at Aaron's wall clock when I turned to follow the dirty men into the house. There was fifteen minutes to kill until Aaron arrived. He was never late coming home because he knew I would be there ready and waiting with my pussy on a platter for him.

Fifteen minutes. So much could happen in that short amount of time. My rape, murder, and the mutilation of my corpse were all possibilities. It took everything in me to convince my twisted brain to muster the strength to entertain this hungry-looking pack of wolves.

Based on their wandering eyes alone, they were hungrier for me than they were for food. I may as well have been standing there naked and bent over the couch.

"Have a seat. I made beef stroganoff if you gentlemen are hungry."

Gentlemen. Ha! They were more like a bunch of rabid hellhounds.

"Lady, are you serious? You're the maid and Aaron's personal property? Did Aaron pull you out of one of those nuthouses?"

This was the third or maybe even fourth time someone had accused me of being crazy. The talker bolted in my direction when I took a step toward the kitchen. He gripped my arm hard enough that it would leave a bruise.

He slung me onto the couch next to the shortest beard, mangy, and cold-sore-faced one.

Shortest beard glanced over at me, his cold sore still pulling my attention. I saw the raggedy wheel turning in his head as he side-eyed me. "So, this is how the August Knights get away with fucking black women? Hide them away in their secret homes in the woods?"

What was I supposed to say to that question? I kept my gaze on the carpet as I rubbed my sore arm from where the woman-slinger had gripped it.

"Shit, I am kind of hungry. And that food does smell mighty good. And we've been staking out these damn woods for days trying to figure out where that bastard lived," Cold Sore informed. He absently brushed his hand over his dusty jeans. "Let her up, Clint. I think I'll have me a bite to eat while we wait for Aaron."

Clint, the woman-slinger, leveled a pointed gaze at Mr. Cold Sore.

"I'll go in the kitchen with her and watch her to make sure she doesn't get away or poison us. We may as well enjoy *everything* before we take care of our business." The one I now knew as Clint volunteered this information. He said it all while letting his cold stare walk all over me.

The sinister glint on dirty-long-beard's face as he watched silently across the room confirmed my assumptions. He was the quietest of the three, but his fixed gaze and quiet scrutiny spoke for him. They were here to kill Aaron and me too for being in the way.

The way Clint and Cold Sore kept glancing at my tits and bare legs proved that their intentions weren't just on the business they wanted to take care of with Aaron. Every crime they could possibly commit was certainly in play—robbery, rape, arson, and murder.

Aaron had warned me that my life was in jeopardy every moment I spent around his MC. The second day had been positive proof when I ended up shooting someone to prove myself to the MC and stood by as they took the rest of their rivals *out back*.

I didn't miss that the bearded group with me now all wore guns shoved down the back of their pants. They proudly left them visible in case I tried something I suppose. My mind whirred, and I kept my horror-filled screams locked inside my head.

Clint shoved me repeatedly toward the kitchen. What was up with bikers and shoving women?

Clint watched, more like *hovered*, while I fixed three plates and retrieved a pitcher of lemonade from the refrigerator.

I recalled the various guns I saw hidden throughout the house when I cleaned it. There was one atop the kitchen cabinet across the room from me, but I would need to climb up on the countertop to be able to reach it. There was also one under Aaron's mattress. One of our sex scenes had been so active we'd managed to work it out from its hiding place under the mattress, and it had fallen to the floor. There was another shoved into the couch that Cold Sore sat on. Three damn guns and I couldn't get to any of them.

I handed Clint his plate, but all I wanted to do was smash the glass pitcher of lemonade against the counter and use the jagged edges to slit his throat.

Clint was so busy eye-balling my legs hanging from under Aaron's shirt that it took him a moment to reach for his plate of food.

I stacked the other two plates and the glasses of lemonade on a serving tray and returned to the living room with Clint following. *What I would do for a box of rat poison right now.* There was no need for me to glance back to know that Clint's creepy eyes were glued to my ass.

Once everyone had a plate, I sat in Aaron's chocolate-brown recliner as instructed and proceeded to fold myself into a tight ball, pulling Aaron's shirt until it stretched over my thighs and hid my overexposed legs.

Clint and Cold Sore sat on the beige leather couch, and longest-beard sat on the light brown leather loveseat adjacent to my chair.

Forks scraping plates and loud lip-smacks were the only sounds that filled the living room. All those times I would cook and pray I had a family to feed the food to, but never had I pictured that a bunch of broke-back bikers would be tasting my food.

If I had leverage over these dirty-dick-buzzards, this would be the last meal they would ever eat. The idea of feeding them their last meal almost made me crack a twisted smile.

Cold Sore chewed using his front teeth as his mouth worked aggressively. His back teeth had likely been knocked out or had rotted out.

It was now 5:35 p.m. Aaron should have been pulling up by now, but I didn't hear his truck. Out of all the days he could have been late, he'd chose today.

I didn't wait to be told. I stood and collected the empty dishes, and this time, Cold Sore followed me into the kitchen. He glared at me with lust-heavy eyes as I placed the dishes into the sink. I hadn't missed the not so subtle eyes they were giving each other. They had eaten and now wanted to fuck.

When Cold Sore walked up to me and thrust his dirty pelvis against my ass, I cringed and ground my top teeth into the bottom ones. This was nothing like when Aaron did this to me. All I wanted to do now was stick a long-handle fork in this asshole's eye socket and bath in a tub of lye to get his asshole-smelling stench off me.

The answer as to why I hadn't heard Aaron's truck came in the form of his approaching black boots that crept across the kitchen floor as silent as night. Cold Sore was too busy fantasizing about what he would do to me to notice what captured my attention and put a sinister smile on my lips.

When I greeted the men on the porch earlier, I spotted the dark-colored vehicle that they attempted to hide in the woods, but they hadn't hidden it well enough. Aaron must have spotted the vehicle on the outskirts of his property and snuck in through the back way.

Click.

Click.

The tip of Aaron's gun against his temple made Cold Sore's breath hitch before he froze. His stiff dick, however, continued to stab into my right ass cheek.

Aaron's voice was low, but the deadly intent that spewed from it was loud and alarmingly clear.

"Back away from her before I blow your brains all over this fucking kitchen."

Cold Sore's hands went up as he eased back. "I ah..."

Before he could get the words out, the butt of Aaron's gun struck him in the head. The angry crack upside his head sounded like it had broken through bone. Blood sprayed against my back, and small splatters reached as far as the white blinds before me.

Cold Sore's body hit the floor with a loud thud, but he wasn't out. The assault was impactful enough that his eyes rolled to the back of his head and his eyelids fluttered like wings as he struggled to sit back up.

Aaron's heavy boot thumped upside his head next and took him out.

"Everything all right in there?" one of Cold Sore's dirty buddies shouted from the living room.

Aaron placed a finger to his lips, telling me to stay quiet as approaching footsteps drew closer to the kitchen door.

When Clint stepped into the kitchen and saw Aaron, he immediately drew his gun. He and Aaron were in a standoff, aiming their weapons at each other's heads.

"Chuck! We've got company. Get in here now!" he shouted.

This wasn't going to go well. If only I'd been able to get one of those guns. Aaron was out-numbered, even with one of them knocked out on the floor.

Chuck sprung the door open with his weapon drawn. Since Clint now had backup, he was bold enough to take a few steps past the center island, closer to Aaron and me. He stood next to the refrigerator with his back to the backdoor, blocking the exit. Chuck was blocking the exit to the living room.

We could have jumped over Cold Sore's body and made a run for the back stairs, but it would have likely guaranteed both of us a bullet in the back.

"Aaron, you're outnumbered," Clint stated the obvious.

"What did you do to Dutch?" Clint asked as he glanced over the edge of the table at his fallen buddy laid out at mine and Aaron's feet.

Clint and Aaron kept their standoff going. Their weapons never wavered from each other's heads. I stood in silence, hidden by Aaron's body. Was this my last day on earth?

My already tense body shivered when Chuck shuffled on the other side of the kitchen island and transferred his aim away from Aaron's head to aim it at mine. My heart hammered against my chest cavity, adrenaline lighting my body into an inferno of fear.

"Drop your gun, Aaron, or I'm going to blow your sexy little maid's brains all over that counter."

Aaron refused to drop his gun away from Clint's head, and I could have sworn I saw a smile breeze across his lips. This was that intensely scary part of Aaron that peeked out at me from time to time, reminding me that he was every bit as dangerous as I believed.

"And you are going to watch me, for a second time, kill another one of your sons," he said. His voice dripped with pure venom. He didn't sound like the man I'd been living with for nearly two weeks.

A second time?

I forgot a weapon was aimed at my head. Aaron had killed one of Chuck's sons? So, they weren't here for money or drugs or even guns. They wanted good old-fashioned revenge.

I had managed to survive for nearly a month with a group of bikers, who were known murderers, but here I was standing with a gun aimed at my head. It was the closest I'd come to dying, in the kitchen of one of the bikers I was fucking for nearly two weeks.

Bullet to the head was not the way I wanted to go...not the way *anyone* wanted to die. I wondered which reporter would get to tell my story or if my body would ever be found.

My heart seized in my chest when Chuck leveled his weapon and his finger tightened on the trigger. I slammed my eyes shut, unwilling to see it coming and not wanting to know the moment that signified the end of my life.

"Drop the fucking gun, Aaron or I'm going to kill that bitch right now."

As scared as I was, I knew enough to know the way this world operated. My eyes popped back open. If Aaron dropped that gun, we were dead anyway. At least he had a little leverage aiming his gun at Chuck's son's head.

When Aaron's hand wavered like he was about to drop his weapon, my gaze left the barrel of death in Chuck's hand and landed on Aaron's back. I couldn't believe what I was about to say.

"Aaron, don't drop shit. They will kill us anyway."

Chuck smiled at me. "You got some balls, little maid. I'll give you that much."

I had a compulsive urge to do something stupid. Since our chances of surviving this was slim to none, I went with my stupid impulse.

Just as Chuck's gaze left me and his lips moved to say something else, I reached up and gripped Aaron's strong arm with both of mine and yanked him down to the floor with a hard tug.

CHAPTER SIXTEEN

Megan

We went crashing to the floor. My yank was harder than I assumed it would be since I had put all my weight into it. Aaron landed halfway on top of me and my knee went crashing into Cold Sore's chest.

Aaron didn't need instructions for my stupid plan; he started shooting from our floor-level position, which sent Clint and Chuck back but not away.

The center island, containing the stove and an attached, thick, wooden table were the only things keeping bullets from striking us. I scrambled over Cold Sore's body and poured all my might into turning him over. I grunted as I lifted and shoved at his body. When my eager fingers raked the butt of Cold Sore's gun, I yanked hard to jerk the weapon from under him.

I continued to pull in a panicky hurry as a bullet hit loud, splintering the wood next to me. When I got a good grip on the pistol shoved down the back of Cold Sore's pants, relief swept through me.

I called out to the men shooting. My breath heaved so hard that I didn't know if they understood my words.

"I give up! I'm getting up. *Please*. I'm coming out!"

Unsure if my crazy ploy to come out would work, I noticed the bullets had stopped flying, including Aaron's, when he spotted what was in my hand.

Aaron lifted Cold Sore, still out, his slumped body jerked, and his chest moved up and down. Aaron used the man for cover as we ducked low, behind his crumpled, smelly body.

"Stay behind me, Megan," Aaron directed, as he stood higher, with Cold Sore now groaning in front of us. He leaned Cold Sore's body more so that he was covering me from Chuck although it had already been proven that Chuck wasn't willing to shoot Aaron, not if Aaron had a clear shot of his son.

Chuck and Clint's weapons were waiting for us when we were standing fully upright. Chuck's gun was aimed mostly at Cold Sore instead of me, and Clint and Aaron were back in their standoff.

As soon as Cold Sore began to stir and realized he was a human bulletproof vest, he started to scream like a madman. His voice was laced with horror due to the situation was currently in.

Aaron didn't give a signal and he didn't wait around to see what Chuck and Clint would do. Cold's screams distracted both bearded pieces of shit and Aaron started shooting. His first shot landed in the center of Clint's forehead, spraying blood and brain matter on the refrigerator and wall behind him.

Soon afterward, I stood deathly still with the odor of gun oil inching up my nose. The same as how it had done in Shark's bar the second day I was with The August Knights Motorcycle Club.

The gun in my hand remained aimed where Chuck had been standing a moment ago. I believe I shot him at least three times and my finger kept squeezing the trigger until the gun stopped firing. My next breath got caught up in my throat when I realized what I'd done. My gaze moved away from where Chuck was standing, in time for me to see Aaron raising his gun and putting a bullet in the back of Cold Sore's head.

The sound of the *boom* so close left both my ears ringing, but I preferred the ringing to Cold Sore's incessant screams. The sudden silence allowed my brain to reflect on the deadly moment I had just survived.

I was stunned and frozen in place, not believing I was in one piece. My rapidly blinking eyes were the only movement I was capable of making at the moment.

After Cold Sore's lifeless body hit the floor, Aaron spun quickly to check me out. His frantic hands brushed over my body, searching for bullet holes.

"Are you shot?" he asked, his voice revealing the first hints of panic.

It hadn't occurred to me until Aaron's question that Chuck and Clint had enough time to shoot Aaron and me. I wasn't sure if it was fear or their arrogance that kept them from firing on us earlier, but I was grateful.

Aaron took the gun from my hand and placed it on the counter behind us. I glanced down at myself, expecting to see a hole through a part of me. I swept my hands over my chest with quick movements. Aside from Cold Sore's splattered blood, there was no sign that I was shot or was losing any blood.

I snapped back to reality when I noticed Aaron's injury.

"Shit! They got you."

Aaron caught my hands and gripped them firmly inside his. Mine were shaking like crazy, but his was perfectly calm.

"Trust me, this is nothing but a flesh wound. I'll get you to patch me up later."

The wound was a nick across his neck that resembled a knife wound more than a bullet graze. There wasn't much blood, so I calmed enough to think. I closed my eyes and took a much-needed deep breath before Aaron drew me against his solid chest. I settled into his embrace, throwing my arms around his torso as I buried my face in his strong chest.

"I'm sorry you had to witness and participate in this shit," he said, not sounding the least bit remorseful. "This is what I was trying to make you understand about the kind of people you were getting yourself involved with."

I recovered enough to think more clearly. Glancing up at Aaron while wrapped in his arms, I mouthed the last words I'm sure he didn't expect to hear from me.

"I know you can't call the cops, so I'll help you clean this up."

He squinted, but he didn't reply.

"Can you give me the full story of why these guys wanted to kill you and how you came to kill Chuck and now both of his sons?"

Most people never considered that there were writers who took their work as seriously as reporters. Some were willing to go into the belly of the beast if it meant finding a decent enough story to write or report about or to gain first-hand knowledge, insight, and ideas.

However, the jury was still out on me. I didn't know if I was just plain crazy or if Aaron had been right all along. Maybe I got off on being scared. Nevertheless, there was no way I was not going to use the gruesome action I witnessed in my time with The August Knights Motorcycle Club in my upcoming books. Infiltrating this MC had given me a lot more than I bargained for and I was still alive to pen all the gory details.

Aaron didn't hide the twinge of dismay that flashed into his gaze. He opened and closed his mouth a few times, unsure of what to say to me as his gaze searched mine.

I explained, "I'm a writer. As crazy as it may sound to you, I just witnessed and survived enough to find a way to turn it into two or three bestsellers. I literally just stared death in the face and lived to talk about it. I can't let something so astounding go to waste."

Aaron's hands dropped away from me at this point. He started like he was just seeing the real me for the first time. I believe my words unnerved him more than the dead bodies on his kitchen floor.

He stared at me and down at the bodies alternately like he was deciding which was worse—my ability to handle a kitchen full of dead bodies or his actual kitchen full of dead bodies.

He unconsciously tapped me on my ass, and as much as I hated to admit it with dead bodies at my feet, I liked it. A moment ago, I was scared out of my twisted mind, but now that I was over the shock of it all, I was fine. The shaking had stopped, and my brain was like a revved engine stuck on the highest gear.

"Gather all the cleaning supplies, mop, and bucket, and all the bleach we have in the house. I have more supplies in the storage shed that I need to go out and grab."

I guess that meant that he'd decided to take me up on my offer to help him clean up. However, he didn't comment on the exclusive I asked him for, on his involvement with Chuck.

***

I paused when Aaron entered the kitchen. He had gone up the back stairs and through the living room and back since both exits out of the kitchen were blocked by dead bodies.

He carried what I assumed was acid. He placed the two gallon-sized jugs on the counter along with a stack of rags he'd had shoved under his arms.

The dead men on his floor weren't as interesting as he found me right now. Once he sat down the supplies, he stepped closer to his side of the counter and leaned over, eyeing me suspiciously. He pinned me with a gaze I couldn't read, studying me.

"What are you doing, Megan?"

What could I say? He'd caught me standing over a dead body, studying it. I was interested to see where I had shot Chuck since it seemed I was in a daze when I pulled the trigger. Of course, I couldn't tell Aaron why I was standing over the dead man.

"Seeing all we'll have to clean," I answered, lying.

"Come here." Aaron beckoned me closer with a commanding finger.

I stepped away from Chuck's lifeless body and walked over Clint's to get to Aaron as Cold Sore's dead eyes stared at us from the other direction.

"Yes?"

He gripped my shoulders, pulling me closer. "You know. I assumed that you were in shock earlier when you started talking about writing at a time like this. But, I was wrong, wasn't I?"

He didn't give me time to answer his question.

"You aren't shocked at all. This excites you, and I think you're just as fucking bat-shit crazy as me because watching you take all this crazy shit with ease has my fucking dick harder than a brick."

My nipples hardened at his words and pressed against the soft fabric of his T-shirt. The sound of his voice, so hungry for me, made my pussy clench hard. Nothing more needed to be said. I reached down and palmed Aaron's dick hard. The action caused him to take a deep sip of air as his mouth dropped open.

A second later, I was being hoisted on top of the table as Aaron proceeded to rip my underwear off. Despite all that had happened, I still hadn't put on any pants or shoes. My legs were bruised from the fall we had taken on top of Cold Sore, and my arm and elbow were all scraped and battered, but I didn't care.

All I could do was gasp when Aaron tugged down his pants and shoved his long, thick dick into my slick pussy with a hard thrust that reached clean to the back of me. Aaron's powerful legs slapped against my inner thighs as the *thump* of the rocking table under our weight echoed over the dead silence of our audience.

We were so turned on and excited that it seemed like it only took minutes for us to reach our peak. I came so hard my vision swam, and lightheadedness caused me to wobble before I exploded into a cloud of brilliant sensation. Aaron's loud roar as he came inside me probably scared animals roaming outside in the woods.

After we came down from whatever sick and twisted thrill that had taken our minds, I finally threw on my pants and prepared to start the task at hand.

CHAPTER SEVENTEEN

Megan

It had been a long ass day. After Aaron and I calmed ourselves enough to function, we began the process of cleaning his kitchen.

I glanced at Aaron. "I've been around enough dead bodies not to be squeamish around them, but I've never had to get rid of one. You're going to have to instruct me on the best way to go about this."

Did he just smile?

"First, I'll need you to help me clear these bodies out of here."

That sounded easy enough. "Okay," I said as I took in the display of bodies in front of me.

Chuck was thrown back against the wall and door that separated the kitchen from the living room. His damaged head and hunched shoulders were slung against the wall, and his lower body was twisted away from his top half. It was like he was two different parts, trying to make up one body.

His bladder and bowel movement was In a brown puddle of liquid around the twisted lower half of his body. The scent seeped into my nose and made me want to gag, but I swallowed the gut-turning impulse and ignored the stench.

Although Chuck was shot in the head, I didn't see much brain matter against the wall. But there was a significant amount of blood spatter that needed to be cleaned. A large pool of blood also sat under his slumped body and threatened to meet the brown pool of piss.

Cold Sore, who I vaguely recalled Chuck calling Dutch was on his stomach on the floor where Aaron had dropped him. A large chunk of the back of his head was blown off, and an unnatural scent crept up my nose and gripped my throat. It was the scent of the inside of his head. It was like shit, rotted food, and vomit that had sat in the sun all day. Not at all something you wanted to be near for long periods of time.

I burped when my lunch began inching up my throat. Most of Dutch's brain matter had hit the floor and a portion had landed on the counter in front of him. His fists were clenched tight like he'd lived for a few moments after his fatal shot and he was fighting to cling to his last few seconds of life. One of his legs was bent in an L-shape like he might attempt to get up. His head was twisted far enough up that I could easily see his open, lifeless eyes.

Clint had the most dramatic display in my opinion. He was the type of dead body you'd see outlined in chalk and used to scare teens away from the dangers of guns and drugs.

He was laid flat out on his back. His arms and legs were splayed away from his body. Pieces of his skull and hunks of brain matter were splattered against the

TWISTED MINDS · 159

refrigerator, painting its snow-white surface with dark red splatters and spots.

Clint's eyes and mouth were wide open like he saw the bullet traveling toward his head and had frozen in wide-eyed, open-mouthed shock. The bullet must have killed him on impact because his body had fallen straight back into the path near the back door.

I took each man by the feet as Aaron and I carried them to his backyard. The back porch light was bright enough to guide us along our twisted path. The moon hovered low in the sky like a living creature, peeking from behind the clouds at the twisted shit Aaron and I were doing.

Even the insect calls sounded ominous. Instead of night songs, it was night wails, like they were bearing witness to something they knew they weren't supposed to see.

We sat the bodies in a pile next to one of those thick metal tubs that animals used for drinking water. Aaron poured in one of the jugs of acid. Smoke billowed and hissed out of the big metal tub as the dangerous liquid created a bubbling sound. Aaron gripped my wrist and pulled me away from the fumes.

"We should be wearing a mask around this shit. Try not to breathe any of it in. I'll grab us something to cover our faces with."

Once Aaron was out of sight, I stood in his backyard with the three bodies that were about to be soaked in acid. I took in the metal tub of acid and the bodies stacked beside it. Glancing back and forth, I waited for sympathy or even regret to show up. It didn't.

Had my heart gone completely black? Had I lost my grip on reality? Was I so broken that I could no longer produce the emotions of a normal person?

Aaron returned. He stood behind me and tied a black handkerchief over my mouth and nose. Once he'd secured his, we resembled two outlaws. Was an outlaw what I had become?

Once I helped Aaron roll the bodies into the acid, I stood, watching him watch the bodies. Eventually, I learned that he wasn't just watching, he was waiting to turn the bodies so that the acid would eat at every part of them. He turned and poked the bodies with a large wooden boat paddle.

Aaron remained outside to make sure the bodies were cooked evenly as I re-entered the house to finish the process of cleaning the kitchen.

By the time Aaron walked into the kitchen, I had cleaned it so well you'd never have known that three bodies had been splayed out all over the walls and floor. Aaron raised an approving eyebrow as he glanced around the space.

Clumsily maneuvering a pair of vice grips, I attempted to yank a bullet free that had gotten lodged in the wall. Once it was freed, I noticed blood on it, which meant that it had traveled through Chuck's body. I recalled pulling the trigger multiple times, but I didn't know how many times I shot Chuck until after I observed his body. When Aaron caught me lingering over his body earlier, it was a part of what I was attempting to figure out.

"I'm about to take them out back," Aaron said as he pointed a thumb over his shoulder.

There were those words again. *Out back.* Frankly, I assumed they were already out back. This time, I wanted to see what *out back* looked like. I wanted to see what *out back* meant to this MC.

"Can I go with you?" I asked, trying not to sound too curious.

Aaron shrugged nonchalantly. "Okay."

I dropped the vice grips and bullet onto the paper plate I was using to collect bullets and shell casings on. Aaron glanced at the plate and back at me, but he didn't comment. He seemed puzzled at how well I was handling what normal people might have considered a nightmare.

Once I stepped into the backyard, I lifted my handkerchief over my mouth and nose and peeked inside the tub. My mouth dropped open behind the handkerchief at seeing three bodies reduced to a giant tub of chunky soup. There were chunks as large as sides of beef, but I doubted that any of these men could be identified by what was left of them. Did acid eat away the teeth and bones too? I wanted to ask Aaron, but I believed I'd hit my quota of weird shit to ask him.

I had spotted the two motorcycles Aaron kept inside his garage due to him setting my treadmill up in the area. However, I'd had no idea what he kept in the small shed behind his house that was always locked until tonight. It was where he kept the four-wheeler and his killing supplies. His man cave slash kill house, I suppose.

Aaron hooked the wheeled metal tub of chunky human soup to the back of his four-wheeler. He secured a large metal door over the tub to keep the toxic contents from splashing out. Once he accomplished that task, he climbed onto the four-wheeler and patted the area behind him on the seat. I hopped onto the back of the ATV with him.

We drove deep into the crowded, dark depths of wavy trees. I sat behind Aaron on the humming motorized vehicle, hugging his waist like we were on a dark date that twisted minds like ours would enjoy. Occasionally, I glanced back at the tub of sloshing flesh bouncing behind us. Although Aaron had covered it, I could still hear the slushy mess inside the tub over the buzzing engine of the ATV.

Aaron instructed me to remain seated as I watched him dig a hole as deep as his shoulders and as wide as one of his outstretched arms. There was likely an easier way to do this, but I got the impression that he liked the physical labor involved with doing it his way.

A large lantern that hung from the handlebar of the ATV provided enough light for Aaron to complete his task. It was obvious he had done this before. All the equipment he needed to get rid of a body was at his house, readily available. He also knew where to take the bodies and where to dig.

He removed the metal, makeshift door he used to cover the bodies. The tub was affixed to a small carry trailer, built with a sliding mechanism that allowed the tub to lift so he could dump the soupy contents into the hole with ease.

After everything was dumped and the tub was back in place, Aaron began the task of covering Chuck, Clint, and Dutch's remains with dirt. Again, I waited to feel remorse in light of what was taking place, but it never came.

CHAPTER EIGHTEEN

Megan

After peeling myself away from Aaron's chest, I turned off the blaring alarm clock. It was 2:30 a.m. We needed to get dressed so that we could use the cover of darkness to get rid of Chuck's vehicle. Aaron had parked the truck behind his house until it was time for us to get up and get rid of it.

I followed Aaron, who was driving Chuck's blue heavy-duty truck. I marked off another day in my head. This was day twenty-nine in my thirty-day ride with the August Knights Motorcycle Club.

I'd received a lot more than I bargained for as it dealt with the level of violence this group was capable of conjuring up and dispensing. I had shot one man in the shoulder as well as shot and killed another. Death had walked up to me, and I stared it in the face. Not only that, I was willfully carrying on a sexual relationship with one of the MC's chairmen.

After hours of driving, we crossed the Florida state line and entered the state of Alabama. Aaron stopped to refuel and to take a bathroom break. Before we got back on the road, he hopped into his truck with me, sitting on the passenger's side.

"I want to get Chuck's vehicle as far away from Florida as possible. Let's head up north into the mountains of Tennessee. I know a place where I can roll it over a cliff into the water."

Already dirt-deep into the shit, I nodded. "Sounds like a good plan to me," I agreed, flashing a smile.

I believe me being able to handle the aftermath of so much death without showing remorse impressed him. It wasn't obvious in his actions but this was a new endeavor for Aaron, having a non-club member he could share his dirty deeds with.

We fell silent for a few seconds before a smile slid across my lips. I wasn't smiling because of his suggestion. Just looking at him sent my hormones jumping. The man emitted sex appeal like he sprayed it on. On the rare occasion he released a smile, any female within sight would be in deep trouble. He never attempted to be sexy or seductive—he just was.

To my surprise, Aaron leaned over his center console and placed a sweet kiss on my cheek before exiting the vehicle. I glanced around the area. Anyone could have seen us, but it occurred to me that Aaron didn't care about people's opinions.

If I was reading him right, I believe he was developing feelings. Shit, I developed them as soon as he stroked my body, but I had enough sense to know that we were always one screw away from our end.

A wide grin lit my face when I recalled a number of the sexual episodes I experienced with Aaron. He lived a life outside the law, and although I was starting not to want to, I needed to get back to my reclusive and nomadic life of writing books.

However twisted, living this adventure with Aaron was one of the very few highlights of my life. Although I chose to live a sheltered life now, it hadn't always been that way.

My life as a foster care kid had been a hellish anarchy of violence and crime that had twisted my mind into so many knots it would be entwined for the rest of my life.

***

Six more hours and another pit stop brought us to the area Aaron had picked out. I watched him wipe down Chuck's truck with a dusty white rag he found in the tackle box.

He leaned under the open driver's side door into the vehicle and did something to the brake and accelerator before he stood behind the truck and attempted to shove it forward. His boots scratched up rocks and dirt and several loud grunts sounded before the truck began to roll.

At first, it moved at a sluggish pace before picking up enough momentum to teeter over the cliff. The scene was like watching a clip from a movie.

Hurrying from behind the wheel of Aaron's truck, I climbed out in time to see the ass end of Chuck's truck careen over the side of the rocky bank. My gaze remained glued to the scene. The sound of twisting metal sounded off as gravity sucked the truck down and sent it hurtling into the dark grayish-blue water below.

The truck didn't go down the rocky bank easily. It scratched and clawed against the jagged sides of the mountain all the way down. The windows were left rolled down, and the back window remained open. When it finally hit the water, it sank, bubbling to the bottom of the waving dark bed of liquid.

On our return trip, I reclined the passenger's seat and napped most of our drive back to Aaron's house. When we drove into his yard around six that evening, we found his father sitting in the yard inside his truck with the motor running.

Shark's fingers drummed against his steering wheel as he eyed Aaron and me suspiciously. His door screeched when he finally exited his vehicle.

I purposely remained in the background as father and son stopped and chatted on the porch. Aaron gave Shark the quick version of what had taken place inside his house and where we had just returned from. Shark's eyes flashed a small crease of concern, but it was easy to see he had a lot of confidence in his son's ability to take care of himself.

When Aaron relayed the part I played in taking out Chuck and his crew, Shark's long, lazy stare unnerved me. He was taking a deep enough look to see the real me for the first time, his expression similar to how Aaron had stared me down in his kitchen last night.

Shark's gaze remained on me, but his words were meant for Aaron. His forehead creased like he was having a hard time deciding something. His eyes squinted as he continued studying son and me.

"Son, you know I'm a man of my word. Martha's thirty days are up tomorrow. I think she's proven that she can be trusted. Do you want me to take her where she needs to go and drop her off or do you want to do it?"

He didn't say *out back*, so I supposed it meant Shark hadn't decided to kill me. Although I believe I did enough to earn the MC's trust, I had to consider that I had also seen and learned enough about their MC business that it wouldn't be a stretch for them to still want to put a bullet in my head.

Aaron frowned, glancing from his father to me, just realizing our time had come to an end.

"I'll take her," Aaron said, his voice tight.

Shark turned toward me. "Consider your sister's debt paid. I'll put the word out to the MC that they are to leave her crack head-ass alone. What is her name again?"

Shark not being able to remember mine or my sister's name was not reassuring, considering I'd worked a month for the MC for that sole purpose.

"My name is *Megan*, not Martha, and my sister's name is *Jennifer*. Thank you for keeping your word."

Shark nodded and gave me a strange look before waving back at his son and hiking back to his truck. I think he sensed something was off the way he kept glancing back at Aaron and me.

***

Before cooking the last meal I would make for Aaron, I took a long hot shower. His face was droopy, and he was quieter than usual. Was he going to miss me? Men like him didn't miss women. They usually had a line of them waiting their turn.

When I handed him his second beer, he gripped my hand after transferring and setting the beer on the small table next to him. We sat there with him gripping my wrist until he made the decision to pull me onto his lap. I readjusted and straddled his legs, inching my pelvis closer to his although I didn't think his intention was for sex.

His heavy gaze searched my face as his hands massaged my thigh and lower back. He reached up and brushed an escaped curl from my face.

Emotions he fought to keep hidden peeked through the strained lines of his handsome face and poured from his eyes. There was an uprising of unchecked feelings swirling though my system, ones I didn't expect and was not prepared to deal with.

"You're so fucking beautiful, Megan."

My lips fell apart and I stilled. I wasn't much of a talker, but his unexpected compliment left me speechless. He noticed. He gave me a soft peck on the lips and drew back to glance into my face.

His penetrating emotion-filled gaze scared the shit out of me. This was not the Aaron I believed I knew. He wasn't soft and sensual and careful.

However, it seemed he was attempting to be careful with whatever he was about to tell me. Please God, not the L-word. Not with Aaron. Not right now. Not with me. I was too messed up. Too complicated and twisted. And so was he.

"I have to be honest with you," he said with a pinched brow. "The news about tomorrow being your last day has my mind all fucked up."

Relief swept through me. It wasn't that dreaded L-bomb, but it was nearly as bad. What the hell was I supposed to say after the mention of my last day? We were supposed to be fucking, not feeling. However, when it came to Aaron, no matter how much I thought one thing, my damn mouth said something different.

"I know. It was all I could think about on the drive back."

Aaron kissed me hard. His urgent lips crashed into mine as his strong tongue wrap circles around the slippery contours of mine. After a moment, the harshness of the kiss died, and it began to soften and become delicate and slow.

I drew back, eyeing Aaron like I didn't know who the hell I was kissing. This was not his way. This shit was scary in a way that it had me jittery and eager to jump out of his lap. He couldn't even hold my eye contact. His head landed on my shoulder as he tugged me into him, gripping me like he wasn't ever going to see me again.

Truth was, he *wasn't* going to see me again. Was this his goodbye? I was not good with goodbyes.

Goodbyes fucked with your head. He'd just admitted as much a moment ago. Goodbyes had you doubting what you already made up your mind to do. I couldn't let anything sway me from doing what I knew needed to be done. I needed to get back to my quest of survival and resume my life.

"Stay a few more days," he uttered the statement into my neck, barely above a whisper.

I drew back, searching his eyes. "No," I said, surprising myself as much as I believed I surprised him.

His jaw tightened at my rejection. I shook my head, attempting to rid it of the self-doubt creeping in. My eyes pinched as I stared into his, fighting to be strong when all I wanted to do was give in to his request.

His tight jaw and the stressed lines around his sad eyes spiked my need to explain myself.

"I hate goodbyes even worse than I hate dragging them out. We should rip the Band-Aid off and get it over with. You drop me off at the airport and let that be it. I had the best sex of my life with you, fun moments, murderous moments, an all-around whirlwind adventure, but I have a life I need to get back to, and so do you."

He didn't say anything. He only stared at me and considered my words. His left eye twitched and his expression was almost painful like he was having a hard time accepting the reality of our situation.

"Fuck. You're right." He shook his head, fighting to accept what I was saying.

I reminded him, "If you think I'd ever tell anyone about what happened here, I won't. I participated too. Killed someone too, and I don't feel bad about it, considering they hunted you down to come and kill you."

He kissed me after those words, with such tender and delicate ease that it was like I was kissing an entirely different person. My damn insides were fluttering like crazy, and there was nothing I could do to stop it.

This kiss…

It was filled to the brim with pure, raw, uncut emotion; the kind of emotion that scared the shit out of you. It was the kind of intoxicating kiss that reached into me with a depth that gripped my heart and wouldn't let go. It was the kind that made you do dumb shit.

This much emotion didn't belong to Aaron and me. It wasn't supposed to be possible.

He drew back, breathing harshly. When he looked at me this time, I didn't miss it. Right there in his eyes. My eyebrows shot up so fast I'm sure they landed at the top of my hairline.

Aaron jumped up and almost sent me tumbling to the floor, but he gripped my wrists in time to keep me from falling.

"I need to get some fucking air. For fuck's sake, I can't take this shit," he barked, shaking his head like he were attempting to shake off whatever had climbed into his body.

He dropped my wrists and shivered before he took off toward his front door. I understood what he meant about not being able to take it because I couldn't move. I remained in place, shaking and staring at the door. The level of emotions he'd dredged up in me scared me shitless and excited me at the same damn time.

When Aaron returned two hours later, we ate and talked about everything except what was so obvious between us. Had it been there, hidden between us the entire time?

We fooled ourselves into thinking we could fuck without emotion, ignore the strong chemistry between us, and move on without being affected. We'd been so fuck-ing wrong that the truth of our situation was drowning us.

Later that night, Aaron fucked me into oblivion, and he fucked me some more after he decided that oblivion wasn't enough. By the time we fell asleep, it was after 2:00 a.m., and I was having a fucking crisis of conscience.

A part of me wanted to stay with Aaron, but the part of me that made the hard decisions won the battle. I had to leave. I was in more trouble than Aaron or this MC could even imagine. They were bad people, some of the worst I had encountered. However, Aaron was why I needed to put distance between us. I cared about him way too much to lead my trouble to his doorstep.

CHAPTER NINETEEN

Aaron

Sleep didn't come easy last night even after I fucked myself into what I assumed was a minor coma. The idea of Megan leaving didn't sit well no matter how much I attempted to convince myself otherwise.

I'd developed feelings for her…feelings I never had for any other woman. They were feelings I didn't even think I could produce.

I didn't have to reach to know that Megan wasn't in bed anymore. I sensed the emptiness before I lifted my head.

She was likely making me breakfast for the last time. She was one of the most extraordinary women I'd ever met. There weren't many women who could take the kind of murder and mayhem that usually revolved around my life. Not only did Megan prove that she could take it, but she was also capable of dishing it out.

It should have been me in that tub of acid and in that grave in the woods instead of Chuck, Clint, and Dutch. If Megan hadn't been brave enough to pull that suicidal shit and react against two men with guns intent on killing us, we'd likely be dead. She had saved my life.

My father said she also saved Wade's life by shooting Scud. Did she have any idea the level of respect she'd earned from my MC in such a short time? Maybe I saw what I wanted to see in my father, but when my father found out she saved my life, I could have sworn pride flashed in his eyes.

Megan was the kind of woman I'd been searching for my entire life and today would be the last day I spend with her. All these years it seemed that no woman was ever good enough for me and could never fully satisfy me the way I wanted. None had ever understood my personality. Megan did. She fit. She made sense to me. She understood me. Of the little I knew about her, I knew her well enough to know that once she left, she wasn't coming back, no matter what kind of feelings were swimming between us.

I crept down to the kitchen and like I thought, she'd made me breakfast. Where the hell was she, though? She was nowhere in sight. I stood there for a frozen moment, glancing around my empty kitchen that gave off the scent of cleaning products beyond the aroma of bacon and eggs.

When I stepped past the table, a chill rode me so hard I shrugged my shoulders attempting to roll it away. The silence in my house grew more intense the longer I searched and didn't see Megan.

Her phone was gone. The guest room she only slept in for two nights of her fifteen-day stay was clean and empty. Her backpack was not in the living room closet. No trace of her was left.

She was gone. I knew it. I sensed it. But, dammit, I didn't want to accept it.

When I stepped onto my porch, my gaze ran past my parked truck and panned around to the woods that surrounded my place, particularly the area I informed her was eight miles in the direction of the town.

"She fucking didn't." The words flew past my lips as my feet bounded the steps. A dusty gust of wind came out of nowhere and swept against me as I skittered over sticks, rocks, and dirt. I was headed toward the eight-mile stretch of densely populated woods.

Megan had expressed to me that running was one of her most well-liked hobbies. I'd seen her run, ten, twelve, and even fourteen miles on that damn treadmill. If she wanted to get away from me, she was in damn good enough shape to leave whenever she wanted.

It didn't take me but a minute to find the disturbed earth, broken twigs below my shoulder level, and a few broken branches that she'd stepped on. She damn sure wasn't kidding about not wanting to say goodbye.

My first instinct was to hop in my truck and see if I could track her to town, but I discarded the idea. She was right. We needed to rip the Band-Aid off. Nothing good would come of us attempting to forge something that wasn't meant to be.

I sat on my steps and stared at that stretch of woods for an hour. My earlobes tingled to have her whispering her motivating curse words into my ear, telling me how good I was fucking her. My fingers ached to touch any part of her lush and intoxicating body.

The sight of all that soft and silky brown skin had turned me on like nothing else ever had. My nostrils flared for a remnant of her sweet scent. My tongue skimmed across my lips, imagining it were her juices passing over them to rain all over my tongue. My dick throbbed, aching to sink into her magical pussy.

I sat there, waiting, I suppose, for her to change her mind and come out of those woods. The fucking insects and birds teased me with their buzzing melodies as they sat high in the trees.

She had fucking left, disappeared like she'd never existed. The longer I sat, the angrier I became. The darkness that constantly lingered at my back loomed, taunting and laughing at me too.

A devilish smile inched across my lips as I leveled my daring gaze at those woods. I was the one the MC called on when they needed someone found. Therefore, if I really wanted to, I could find Megan.

I hadn't had time to figure out all her secrets. I hadn't had time to figure out what she'd been hiding from me. At some point I accepted that she was becoming more than just the best sex of my life. It made me notice little things I overlooked before, like how often she avoided talking about herself. I saw the way she skirted the subject of her past.

"I'm not fucking through with you, Megan." The need to find Megan had risen in me just as fiercely as the need to fuck her had taken over my mind. Was I about to make a mistake going after her? Probably, but I didn't give a fuck.

EPILOGUE

The way I left Aaron was cowardly, but there was no way I was sticking around so he could convince me to stay. I was never more addicted to anything than I was to that man.

Then there was his father, the way he glared at me yesterday, and the way he could never remember my damn name, like saying it would make me a real person in his eyes. I got the impression that Shark had never intended to let me go. I believed the only place he ever intended to take me was *out back*.

If Shark's intentions were to harm me, I don't believe Aaron would have let him, but I wasn't sticking around to test my theory. Even as I jogged through the woods, I was unable to focus on what I needed to do because thoughts of Aaron kept swimming around into my damn brain.

I paused and observed the gravesite of Chuck, Clint, and Dutch. The ground and dirt were darker, disturbed, and freshly turned, but if there was one thing I learned, it was that these woods didn't see much traffic. Within weeks, the disturbed earth would probably be covered with twigs, new grass growth, and leaves like nothing had ever happened.

I had been learning my way through these woods while Aaron was at work. I knew how to get to town and had plotted an alternate trail in case Aaron came looking for me.

Having been previously married to a military man had its privileges. Not only had my husband taught me how to handle multiple weapons, but he'd also taught me basic survival skills and how to navigate my way out of wooded areas such as these. I wasn't Bear Grylls kind of good, but I could survive.

In the last three years, I went from California to Maine to Virginia to Kansas to Seattle, and now Florida. I hadn't worked up the nerves to leave the country, but after a month in Copper County, I believe it was time I did. Of all the places I'd lived in the last three years, Florida was my favorite. Obviously, because of Aaron.

But now, it was time for me to move before my past caught up with me. The depths of my tortured past knew no bounds and was laced with demons that were capable of devouring anyone and everything it touched, even a MC as dangerous as the August Knights.

I never expected to care about another man after my husband, but Aaron had gotten to me like no one ever had before. I cared about Aaron. Hell, I may even be in love with him, but the last thing I wanted was for him to get tangled up in my dangerous past, one I've been running from since I was fourteen.

Sure, Aaron lived a dangerous life, but my past was so twisted, I feared even for him. Killing Chuck hadn't been the first time I'd had to take a life. My problem wasn't that I'd killed before, my problem was who I had killed.

After taking a deep breath, I pressed on. I needed to get back to my condo so I could prepare to move to my next destination of choice. It damn sure wasn't going to be Texas. My ass was wanted in Texas and not by the law. So, I desperately needed to pack my shit and move before my trail was discovered and my past caught up with me.

BONUS EPILOGUE

"Oh shit!" I yelled at the sight of the big black Chevy truck that came to a screeching stop right in front of me. I was at the juncture to the only paved highway that would take me into town.

The window came down.

"Get in!" Shark yelled, not even questioning what I was doing running around in the woods.

Fuck!

Fuck!

Fuck!

I was in a mental battle. Should I keep running or climb into that truck with him. Either way he could kill me, and no one would ever know since we were still so far off the beaten path. That wasn't even the biggest kicker. I was a black woman in the middle of redneck alley. Any number of Shark's friends would have been happy to help him catch me and do whatever twisted shit came into their minds.

Reluctantly, I walked around the front of his truck, snatched the passenger door open and climbed into the cab. Silence filled the space after I slammed the door shut and folded my arms over my chest. The hum of the engine

182 · KETA KENDRIC

sounded and instead of heading deeper into the woods, Shark made a U-turn to head toward the town.

"Are you taking me back to the clubhouse so you can kill me and take me outback?"

He glanced at me, his face pinched, angry.

"If I wanted you dead, you would have been the first day you were stupid enough to come anywhere near us. You should be thanking me for saving your life," he spit out.

"Why did you let me stay? That first day I approached you at the clubhouse? I never imagined you would let me stay."

He didn't answer, but I got a sense even back when we first met that he saw something in me that made him want to help me, even if his way of helping me was as twisted as the situation he'd allowed me to enter.

"You and Aaron, you fucked, didn't you?"

I swallowed hard but didn't answer.

"I knew that you would, I just didn't think he would let it go any further."

I snatched my head around at the statement, my eyes up side his head.

"So, why send me to stay with him? I don't understand."

A long-stilted silence fell between us.

"It's not easy being a father. You want to give your kids everything you didn't have. You want them to be happy. Being raised in this life, one could go their entire life in misery. Despite how I raised Aaron, I love him and if there is any kind of happiness to be had in this fucking miserable life, I want him to have it."

"So, you gave me to your son like I was some kind of Christmas present?"

His head snapped around.

"Take it how the fuck you want to. Besides, you enjoyed yourself. You think I'm fucking blind and didn't see the way you two were around each other, the way you looked at each other. You telling me that you sneaking around in these fucking woods don't have anything to do with you running away because you don't know how to handle what happened between you two?"

He had me there. I didn't have a reply. When I glanced up, we were already at the small airport on the outskirts of their town.

"I want you to get on a plane, and never come back."

I swallowed hard.

"Fucking nod or say yes you understand," he gritted.

"Yes, I understand. I'm never coming back."

I gripped the door and turned to get out, but Shark gripped my opposite wrist before I climbed out.

"If I see your face around these parts ever again. I'll kill you myself."

I snatched my arm away, jumped out of his truck, and slammed the door shut. My middle finger was my goodbye to his mean ass. He screeched away from the curb, cutting off a white Toyota that sent a series of angry honks after him.

Sharks death threat put me on edge, but why had he allowed me into their lives in the first place? He never answered the question.

Aaron was not going to be easy to get over. I already missed him. He'd incited a riot of emotions inside me that could rival the effects of hard drugs. His pull on me, on my emotions, and on my body was a debilitating force. I finally understood what people meant when they said a certain person just did it for them.

Attempting to get over a man like Aaron was going to fuck me up in ways I didn't even want to think about. However, I didn't have a choice. I would have to figure out how to get over Aaron just like I had to figure out how to live my life on a timeline laced with death.

End of Twisted Minds

Excerpt

Twisted Hearts Book #2

Synopsis

Megan: How the hell did he do it? Aaron messed with my mind and twisted up my heart, but my body had never been so splendidly ravaged. Stepping away from the August Knights Motorcycle Club was easy, but leaving Aaron was killing me. Was it crazy of me to want to subject myself to the madness the group stood for because I couldn't shake Aaron's hold on me? I couldn't go back. I had to consider his safety. I couldn't allow my twisted past to go crashing into the turbulent life he led.

Aaron: How the hell did she do it? Megan had cracked my chest open and filled it with a riot of crippling emotions I couldn't shake. Letting Megan go wasn't easy. Was it crazy of me to go chasing her after we agreed that it was over? I had to find her. My infatuation with her didn't leave me any other options. In my quest to find Megan, I discovered that she had secrets, deep dark ones I could have figured out if I hadn't gotten distracted. I would make her tell me what she was hiding in that twisted mind of hers—*or else.*

Chapter One

Aaron

I dealt mainly in the weapons portion of my motorcycle club's illicit business, but as a member of one of the most notorious MC's in Florida, one tended to get involved in and see the harsh reality of the drug side of the business too.

The addicts. I despised them. They were weak, pathetic fucks who let something like a piece of crack or meth control their lives and steal their minds. They stole from their family, killed, cheated, and sold their souls to the devil to chase the temporary glory the drug gave them.

I never understood an addict's mentality. Didn't understand how they let something so insignificant run their lives and lead them to make decisions they never would have otherwise. How could they do just about anything for another taste, another hit, another high? I didn't understand what they got out of it, other than a feeling they loved so much they were willing to do anything to experience it again.

Two weeks had passed since Megan disappeared, walked the fuck right out of my life without so much as uttering a goodbye. I hated her for what she did to me. I hated her for making me feel things for her, with her, and about her.

She had intoxicated my system and filled me with needs I never had before. She made me want her in ways I never even fantasized about. For fuck's sake, I had gotten a checkup so I could fuck her without a condom.

I damn sure didn't tell her that she was the only woman I ever fucked in my adult life without one. She would likely have assumed otherwise. However, when the need had risen inside me, so strongly to have her without anything between us, I needed to satisfy it. Just like I needed to find her now, to satisfy my need to see her, hold her, and fuck her brains out for leaving me.

I had to have her even when my father warned me not to touch her. She ignited my body, stimulated my mind, and delved into my spirit. If it were a sin to lust after someone as badly as I yearned for Megan, then I would shake the devil's hand right before walking my ass through his fiery gates.

The worst part was she made me understand how hardcore addicts suffered when they craved their drug of choice and couldn't get it. Megan had no idea she was a fucking drug to me, a fix I'd gotten used to taking whenever my need became too great.

Fuck, most times, I couldn't even wait until the need for her overcame me. She had me so wide open that I fucked her every moment I could. She was the kind of drug I didn't have to chase because she was so giving and willing and ready whenever I wanted a hit.

Now that I didn't have her, I couldn't think, or sleep or fucking eat a damn thing. Instead of having nightmares about all the poor fuckers I've killed in the past, sweat-drenching dreams about the many ways I had taken her all over my house haunted me. Dreams that left my dick hard enough to cut through metal. Dreams that had me calling out for her when I knew she wouldn't answer. Dreams that left me cold and empty, devoid of the sparks she ignited within me.

I often found myself staring into space when people talked to me, her image filling my head instead of me focusing on what was being said. Nausea overtook me on the third day without her, my body going through withdrawals like nothing I'd ever experienced.

Able now to sort through the haze she left me in and focus, a fucking big-ass red flag I neglected to notice, finally occurred to me. I had no idea who Megan was and where she had gone until she was gone. Her name, Megan Jones, was common, so there was no way I could weed her out of hundreds of thousands of others with the same name.

When I really put effort into my thinking, I realized she had never mentioned what state she was from. Megan had driven up over a month ago in a rental car according to my father, but when it was time for her to leave, she mentioned going to the airport.

I had been fucking the woman for weeks, shared my deepest secrets with her, and killed three men with her, but I didn't *really* know her. For fuck's sake, she helped me bury the bodies, had cleaned the crime scene in my kitchen, and I never bothered to ask her where she was from.

Most women would have been offended, hurt or angry, but not Megan. No, she was different.

She mentioned having a hard life growing up in foster care, but she never bothered to disclose the details on how she became so hardened. A soft innocence added a depth to her outside appearance and made her beautiful to the eyes, but she harbored the same kind of darkness I carried around inside me. There was a seething angry darkness flowing through her that allowed her to endure horrific scenes and violent situations that would have had hardened criminals cowering in a corner.

Megan was like me, twisted up in the head enough that she could look a man in the eye and pull the fucking trigger. She inserted herself into our MC, agreed to work for us to pay off a debt she *claimed* her sister owed us for drugs. Who in their right mind would do something so insane? I'd asked her that question many times and never got a straight answer from her.

A few days after Megan left me, I started questioning my MC about her, gathering any information she might have shared with them. All I found was more questions. No one, including my father, the president of our MC, knew Megan's true identity.

My cousin, Jake, had informed me that he didn't remember her sister, the one she was *supposedly* working the debt off for. My father, Shark, claimed he had checked her background, and I believed him. Despite his backwoods ways, he would never have let Megan anywhere near our inner circle if the story she fed him hadn't checked out.

He insisted that he confirmed with a medical professional that her sister was in the Jefferson Rehabilitation Facility in Alabama, based on information Megan had provided to him. How he got a medical facility to divulge patient information was a trick I would have to learn from him one day.

Although I knew they weren't allowed to reveal patient information, I gave it a try anyway. They wouldn't tell me shit, even when I pretended to be a detective and fed them a fake badge number.

My father called the police station to confirm the two detectives Megan claimed she'd spoken to pending her visit with our MC. She said it was to make them aware of her decision to meet with the August Knights of her own free will.

In the thirty days Megan was a cleaning lady, cook, and bartender for us, she found ways to earn my MC's respect. First, she shot a man who would have killed my Uncle Wade. And a few weeks later, she killed a man inside my kitchen, one who'd come to take my life.

The most shocking revelation of it all was that she was the epitome of what my MC was supposed to hate. We were known for being a racist MC. Even though, in my opinion, most of our views and attitudes were strategic tactics to strike fear into the hearts of rival MC's, gangs, or anyone with the balls enough to test us. Granted, there were members who were racist assholes, but a good number of us lived with the perception because it provided an extra layer of danger to our reputation.

The idea of a black woman getting into our inner circle deep enough for us to freely reveal our secrets to her was incredulous. A fucking miracle. It's just not supposed to happen. To have possibly fallen in love with her wasn't supposed to fucking happen either. My plan today to ditch work to go in search of her was damn sure not supposed to fucking happen.

***

With my phone glued to my ear, I heaved a heavy sigh and rolled my eyes every time I was transferred from one office to the next. One detective's desk to the other, I kept bouncing until I was transferred to someone who *might* be able to help me. I clamped my eyes shut and tuned out most of the detective's monotone statements. He didn't confirm the shit I was asking him about.

"Thank you. Appreciate the time," I said, ending the call, my enthusiasm as flat as the detective's tone.

It was the criminal task force unit in Crock County, Florida. The one Megan claimed she visited before engaging our MC. Neither of the numbers listed on the business cards she gave my father worked and the detectives named on the cards didn't work for that precinct.

As a matter of fact, no one at the precinct knew who the hell the detectives were and had never even heard of Megan Jones. Who the hell had my father talked to when he confirmed Megan's story.

I stared at my phone. Could Megan have masterminded her way into my MC?

A sick feeling in my gut was telling me that her story was all a front. Megan was not who she claimed to be. Had she devised a plan that had allowed her to infiltrate the August Knights? If so, why?

Why would Megan do it? What possible reason could she have for wanting to get in bed with the likes of us? Did she even have a damn sister? It was funny that she hadn't mentioned her sister unless I asked about her.

She'd not called to check on this infamous sister during her stay with me either.

Had Megan pulled off the ultimate scheme? Was she a deep cover agent, willing to do anything to catch her criminal or gather information? Was she working for a rival MC?

She couldn't have been a cop because she killed a man in cold blood right in front of me and hadn't shown a hint of remorse. She also shot a man in front of my father and dozens of MC members.

Was *Megan* even her name? Who was this woman and why was it beginning to feel like me and my MC had been manipulated? She got so close that the idea of what she knew about us scared me, and I didn't scare easily.

When I asked questions about Megan, it stirred suspicions with the rest of my MC. They too were now toying with the idea of how easily they allowed her to manipulate them.

I backed off when the whispers of suspicion began. I didn't need to get them excited. They would go off on a half-cocked witch hunt without knowing the full story.

However, I did feel the need to inform my father since he was the MC's president. All eyes were on me when I pulled up.

"Aaron," someone called out. I shot a head nod in the general direction of the voice, not giving a damn who it belonged to. Stepping inside the clubhouse was no better. They didn't have to be looking directly at me for me to sense them watching.

As soon as I glanced at my father across the room and kept walking to the back, he followed me. He stepped into the board room and pulled the door closed behind him. His cocked gaze remained pinned on me the whole time.

"We need to talk about Meagan."

His ears perked and he sat hard in his chair. It only took me a few minutes to offload my speculations, what I discovered, and that I believed Megan had tricked us.

"Kill her. Hunt her down. You need to kill her, " he said, his voice remained level while ordering me to kill a woman.

"Motherfucking, fuck."

I blew out a long breath while he proceeded to curse for what felt like a straight hour.

"That fucking bitch."

I didn't say a word while Megan became every combination of words that you could successfully use with the word *bitch*. He damned her to the far reaches of hell while I listened and watched, bored.

His ego was so high on the pedestal he propped it up on that having someone get one over on him had him blowing all his gaskets and loosening every screw pining his brain to his skull.

If there was one thing Shark couldn't stand, it was being made a fool of. Neither could I. I just handled it better.

Me? I was patient enough to figure out the truth. I would dig until I found answers or found Megan, whichever came first.

Now, I cursed myself for saying anything to my father before I found out the full story behind my speculations. It vexed the hell out of me that none of us knew who Megan truly was or where she came from other than what she'd divulged to us. It proved that I was just as possessed by the glamour she used on us as everyone else.

Shark pounded his fist into the table, making the solid wood vibrate. I left him to his tantrum and allowed my mind to drift.

Where the hell had she gone? We didn't even know where she came from. The only thing I believed at this point was that she truly was a writer. She had written a full manuscript when we were together, and the writing style matched that of her books I'd downloaded and read.

Therefore, I believed one way of tracking Megan down was by her books. I'd read three of them so far including the rough draft of the manuscript she wrote while with me.

In the books that I read, I noticed she left her social media contact information in the back for her readers to interact with her. Those contacts might be my only shot at tracking her down.

I stood, eyeing my father who wasn't cursing but still very, much hot.

"I have a few things to take care of. This stays between me and you."

He nodded, and the last thing I saw before I stepped away was his face drawn into a tight angry knot.

Chapter Two

Aaron

After my first few attempts at tracking Megan down failed, I realized that I would need help. The idea that she might have tricked me and my MC in some way for some reason, was starting to curb the sexual ache and need I had for her.

I even went as far as to send her several emails using the contact information in the back of her books, but she didn't take the bait. Instead, she thanked me for reading her books and offered to send me a free copy of any of her books I hadn't read yet.

My phone vibrated in my pocket, snatching me away from the ideas swirling in my head. It was my friend, D. Derrick Michaels was a computer geek I met and became friends with while in the military. He was no longer in the military, but he offered services that you couldn't readily get on the open market.

D offered the kind of tech services that could send a person to prison for a long time. He presented a quiet, nerdy persona, but I knew better. The man was in my military unit. I'd seen him kill with the same quiet ease in which he lived.

D's services were requested whenever I needed to track down someone. He was a major part of the reason I was able to track enemies for our MC or anyone who convinced themselves that they could hide from me.

Earlier today, I scanned D a copy of Megan's drivers' license. I had taken it from her purse as a security measure, a day after she entered my house. I also gave D her social media information and a listing of all the sites where her books were sold.

"D, what do you have for me?" I asked, forcing a smile over the deep frown on my face as I drove.

A long pause followed the question before D's calm voice flowed through the phone.

"Knox, I got nothing but questions man. Are you sure you want to pursue this woman?"

D called me by my last name, sticking to the way we were trained to address each other in the military.

For him to ask me that question, he must have stumbled upon something that concerned him.

"Yes, I'm sure," I finally answered him. "Why are you asking? What did you find?"

My foot eased off my accelerator a notch, preparing to listen to what D was about to say. I could hear him sigh on the other end of the line.

"That's just it. I didn't find a damn thing. This woman has hidden herself under so many layers that I can't find out who the hell she is, even with a popular writing career. Are you sure she's this writer Megan Jones or was that a cover?"

Confused, I shook my head although D couldn't see it. "Yes. She sat in my house and wrote a full manuscript fast as shit, and from what she let me read, the shit was legit. I was buying it and I don't even read that stuff." I didn't tell D I'd read four of her books, including an unreleased manuscript and had ordered more. Her books gave subtle peeks into her mind, a mind I was sure held more secrets than a confessional.

"She writes under the pen name Megan Jones, but as far as her real name goes, I can't make a connection with a real live person. Hell, for all I've found, Megan Jones could be her real name," D informed me. The hint of concern in his voice wasn't lost on me.

"When I attempted to get into her finances to see where the money from her books sales was going, I discovered that the money goes through an organization called the Phoenix Foundation, which then distributes it to other non-profit organizations."

The crease in my forehead deepened. "What? Are you saying she doesn't use any of the money for herself? How the fuck is she living?" I asked D, aware he hadn't found the answer yet, or he would have told me.

His update had me reeling. Working off a debt for her sister was a fucking rouse if Megan had the ability to give money away. Why did she choose to spend thirty days among my MC?

D continued. "Man, that's one of the questions I've been trying to find answers to. When I hacked into her social media accounts, they were all under Megan Jones, but that was it; no state, city, or anything associated with an actual person. She gives the bare minimum as far as information goes and the details she gives leads to dead ends. All I know is she's someplace in the United States and I ain't even one hundred on that."

When D started using slang terms, I knew something had stumped him. I wasn't sure it was something about himself that he noticed. D was the whitest white boy I knew but had grown up in one of the worst areas in Philly, so he was about as hood as they came. Every now and again, you could hear it in the way he talked.

While there were men who ran around playing hard, D had shared stories of his childhood that rivaled my own. He also saw as much action on the streets of Philly as we saw as soldiers in the active war zones.

"Knox, I can't tell you yet who the hell this Megan is and where the hell she's at, but I'm still searching. The driver's license you scanned me is registered to a legit Texas address. But, Knox, get this shit. When I hacked into the DMV and found the Megan Jones that belonged at that Texas address, it was not the same Megan Jones whose face was on the license you scanned me. Your pretty brown Megan has put her face on a pretty *white* Megan's driver's license."

"What the fuck?" I asked, not believing what I was hearing. Who the fuck had I been sleeping with for two weeks? Who the fuck had I been obsessing over?

These updates had me beyond pissed and so irritated, the vein in my forehead throbbed. Megan had played me. She played my entire MC, pretending to be someone else so she could get whatever the hell she wanted from us. The worst part of the situation was, I still didn't know what the fuck she wanted from us or why.

"I'll keep digging." D's voice lured me away from the dark anger that nipped at my mind and planted deadly intent there. "I have another assignment. It's a field assignment, but I'll work on this for you when I can. I'll call you later to let you know what else I find out."

"Thanks, D," I managed before hanging up. I didn't bother D when he had what he called *field assignments*.

There were times when he went black, and I knew it meant an illegal operation that involved violence and likely death. My fingers clenched tighter around Megan's driver's license. My intentions were to have D check Megan out the day I took her license from her purse, but I got distracted. The sex, the cooking, and her ability to make me feel like I was something special. Even the way she handled the occasional bouts of violence that crept into my life had blinded me to who she was under the surface. Masterfully, she seduced me and made me see only what she wanted me to see.

The driver's license, the only thing I had of hers wasn't truly hers. Hot wasn't a strong enough word to describe me at this point. I wanted to hurt someone. All of that longing and need I'd had for Megan was being eaten away by pure unadulterated rage.

Through gritted teeth, I grumbled at the license in my hand. "When I find you, whoever the fuck you are, I'm going to make you sorry you ever met me."

End of Twisted Hearts Excerpt

Acknowledgement

Bestselling Author was an achievement I accomplished with JWP Publishing. I would like to extend a special Thank You to Publisher and National Bestselling Author, Jessica N. Watkins. I'm eternally grateful to you for originally publishing The Twisted Series. With your vast knowledge of the publishing industry, this series achieved accolades that surpassed my expectations. My appreciation is immeasurable.

Author's Note

Readers, my sincere thank you for reading Twisted Minds. Please leave a review or star rating letting me and others know what you thought of the book. If you enjoyed it or any of my other books, please pass them along to friends or anyone you think would enjoy them too.

Other Titles by Keta Kendric

The Twisted Minds Series:

The Chaos Series:

Stand Alones:

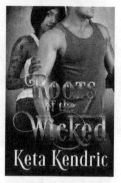

Novellas:

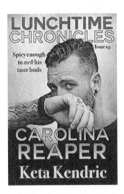

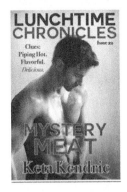

Paranormals:

Kindle Vella:

**Love Lied Series
(Seasons 1-3)**
Keta Kendric

Audiobooks:

Connect on Social Media

Subscribe to my Newsletter or Paranormal Newsletter for exclusive updates on new releases, sneak peeks, and much more.

You can also follow me on:

Instagram:
https://instagram.com/ketakendric

TikTok:
https://www.tiktok.com/@ketakendric?

Bookbub:
https://www.bookbub.com/authors/keta-kendric

Goodreads:
https://www.goodreads.com/user/show/73387641-keta-kendric

Newsletter:
https://mailchi.mp/c5ed185fd868/httpsmailchimp

Facebook Page:
https://www.facebook.com/AuthorKetaKendric

Facebook Readers' Group:
https://www.facebook.com/groups/380642765697205/

Twitter:
https://twitter.com/AuthorKetaK

Pinterest:
https://www.pinterest.com/authorslist/

Made in the USA
Middletown, DE
26 August 2024

59310801R00135